dark desire

ANASTASI FAMILY SYNDICATE
BOOK 2

DORI PULITANO

BEHIND THE BADGE PRESS

"Everyone is a moon and has a dark side, which he never shows to anybody,"

MARK TWAIN

I PACED MASSIMO'S OFFICE, waiting to hear why Matias Silva was on the phone. The Silva's were a well-known syndicate in Chile. They controlled most of the region around there, exporting lithium and various gems. Most of it was legal, but like our own family, some wasn't. We'd dealt with them in the past, helping with the transport of materials to the U.S., but our relationship didn't go beyond that.

So, when he called asking for the patriarch of our family, my hackles rose. The last thing we needed was another issue. We'd spent the last few weeks searching for Antonio. The day someone tried to snatch Catarina from the employee parking lot at the hospital, we thought we almost lost her. The sad truth was we lost Antonio instead. He'd stuck around to talk with the investigator and never made it home. And it took us *hours* to realize something was wrong.

When the family realized he'd been kidnapped, Massimo blamed himself for not taking his absence at our meeting that day seriously. But like the rest of us, we assumed he was tied up with law enforcement, trying to cover the truth behind the attempt on Catarina's life. Instead, he had been taken.

I waited on bated breath as Massimo spoke. When he finally hung up the phone, I stopped pacing and looked at him.

"Well? What did they want?"

"Antonio has been found," Massimo's voice cracked with immense emotion as he spoke. "Matias has him in Chile."

I ground my teeth together, my heart thumping with rage as I listened.

"What the fuck is he doing in Chile?"

"It appears Dmitri Ivanov had him kidnapped and was holding him on Jorge Peru's property. Matias assures me he's safe, but I'll be flying out tonight."

"Dmitri Ivanov?" I didn't try to hide my shock. "The Prizrak?"

"Yes, the Prizrak. Look, Madison is going to want to come with me. Are you going to be okay to stay behind and deal with things here?"

I closed my eyes and sighed. "I'll be fine. Besides, I have Riley to train."

Massimo clicked his tongue. "The new manager?"

"What? You're the one who said I needed help." I could see the tension in his body.

"I know. There's just something about her I don't like."

"Alec cleared her," I said, waving him off. "She's doing fine."

I was irritated I had to hire someone to take over for me, but since Miguel's sister was found dead in my restaurant, I had to resurrect a part of me that prevented me from being at Bellissimo as much. "Let me worry about her. Go get our brother and come home. I'll hold things down here until I hear from you."

"Okay. Vin..." Massimo took a deep breath. "Don't let the darkness take you again. I nearly lost you once. I can't lose you again." He eyed me with deep concern, making me turn away.

When he stepped beside me, I pulled him into a hug before bidding him farewell. Dmitri Ivanov had no idea what he had done. Fucking with the Anastasis was going to be his gravest mistake.

Even if it meant losing myself to bring him down.

one

VINCENZO

My palms twitched with anger as I watched my brother enter the house. His body was battered and bruised, reminding me how close we came to losing him at the hands of Ivanov. I pulled him into an embrace as soon as he was within reach, needing to feel he was real.

"Antonio." My throat tightened with profound guilt and sadness. "I'm glad you're home."

"I'm fine, Brother. Sit down, and I'll fill you in on everything."

For the next several hours, Antonio told us everything he could remember. Blistering, fiery anger coursed through my body as he described how Dmitri took him and how he was now holding his own daughter against her will.

"What are we going to do about it?" I looked at my older brother, who was standing beside a man he'd introduced as Bastian Silva. Dmitri might have been this woman's father, but she was now Matias Silva's heart—and we would stop at nothing to bring her home to him. We owed him that much for saving Antonio.

"We found some information showing he has an estate somewhere outside of Vegas. When we find out where we will pay him a visit," Bastian explained, his English pretty spot on for a man who rarely came to the States.

"Let me know when. I want to be there." I folded my arms across my chest and growled. "This motherfucker is going to pay for everything he has done."

Antonio took a deep breath and looked at Massimo, who nodded.

"There is something else you should know, Vin."

I glanced between my brothers. "What is it?"

"We found evidence that Dmitri is the one who killed Miguel's sister and tried to frame you. We also believe his first attempt at trying to take Catarina was a diversion to get to one of us. I just happened to be the poor schmuck he got first."

I paced the floor, trying to tame the demons inside me. I had to get out of there and let the beast out, or I was going to explode. The darkness I fought was always close to the surface, and hearing Dmitri Ivanov was responsible for everything woke the monster inside. I needed to funnel the anger elsewhere, or it would only lead to bloodshed.

"I need to go. Call me when you have something."

"Vincenzo." Antonio stood slowly and pressed his hand to my back. "Don't do anything stupid. We need you, okay? Let

Massimo and Donny figure out where he is, then you can have your revenge."

"Fine." I nodded my head, covering his hand with mine. "I'm glad you're safe."

Hurrying from the house, I was aware of my siblings' stares. Everyone worried I would succumb to my urges to inflict pain. The only problem was, I already had. Pointing my bike in the club's direction, I knew exactly what I needed. It was the only way to satisfy the need to punish someone without risking something illegal. I quickly returned to the restaurant, ensuring Riley didn't need me, which she didn't—they were about to close up, anyway. Still needing some time to cool off, I rode around the city. It was nearly midnight by the time I pulled into Discoteca.

Fantasia was on the second floor of my brother's club. He'd added it for people with freaky needs like mine. Initially, I was worried he would be embarrassed that I took part in what the club offered, but he understood why I needed the outlet and said nothing. None of my family wanted to see me revert to the monster I'd once been. Stepping into the elevator, I blew out a breath. Everything was spiraling out of control, and I feared I was already losing myself. It wouldn't take much to push me over the threshold that separated me from La Lama.

The metal doors parted, exposing the sleek interior of Fantasia. Inhaling the leather scent, I stepped onto the plush carpet and scanned the room. Holly was behind the bar, serving several of the scantily dressed members. Glancing my way, she smiled and held up a glass, silently asking if I needed a drink. Shaking my head, I walked toward the back office, unnoticed by the patrons. I needed to get out of the clothes I had on and get into character—it was the only way I could utterly lose myself.

Setting my helmet on the desk, I stripped off the leather jacket I wore and tossed it onto the chair, then changed into the leather pants I kept at the club for this very reason. It wasn't hard to find someone willing to submit to my needs. Women usually begged to play with me. Most pretended not to know I was an Anastasi out of respect, or maybe even a little fear. I was one of the most desired Doms in the club. Finding pussy was as easy as snapping my fingers.

"Looking for a submissive tonight?" The timbre voice of Max, another member of the club, grinned as he leaned in and whispered into my ear.

"Yes. You?"

"Nah. I just fucked the hell out of a pretty little brunette. Calling it a night and heading out."

I raised a brow, wondering if she would want another round with me. "Was she any good?"

"She could barely handle me. There's no way she can take what I imagine you want to give tonight." He gave me a knowing grin.

"What makes you say that?"

"The look in your eyes says you want to punish tonight. The girl I just fucked is too new. Tonight was a first for her."

"Yeah. She couldn't handle what I need tonight."

He patted me on the back and jerked his head toward the bar. "Try the redhead."

I looked in the direction he motioned to and saw, hands down, the most stunning woman in the club. It looked like she was wearing a wig, but many people came here in disguise, so that didn't bother me. I didn't want to know them personally—I only wanted their body for the evening.

"Thanks. I'll do that."

Leaving his side, I slid onto the stool beside her and ordered a vodka tonic. I leaned in and whispered into her ear, "You looking for a Dom tonight?"

Her head turned toward me, giving me a glimpse of her piercing green eyes. Like two magnets, they drew me into their depths of mystery. The leather mask did nothing to hide their beauty, only accentuated them.

"Isn't that why most come here?" The rasp of her voice caused my dick to harden as she spun on the stool, scanning my bare chest.

"I like it rough. Can you handle that?"

She ran her palm along the ridge of my muscles and pinched my nipple. Leaning in close, as I had done to her moments ago, she pressed her lips against my ear. The heat of her breath sent a shock wave of desire straight to my cock, making my balls pulse with energy.

"Hard. Rough. Painful." She tugged my hand between her legs. "It's got my pussy wet thinking about it."

My cock strained harder against my pants, threatening to rip open the metal cage holding it in. I stood, taking her hand in mine.

"Let's go."

She followed me into one of the private rooms and shut the door. I walked to the table, pushed it against the back wall, and flicked on the music. The room filled with *Sucker for Pain*, which seemed fitting for what I wanted—*no, needed*—to do to her body.

"Take off your clothes and kneel." I watched in amazement as she stripped off the corset top and leather skirt she was wearing without hesitation.

Already bare beneath the fabric, she dropped to the floor, ready to be commanded. My hands twitched with need. Unlike previous subs, this woman had me enthralled in ways I couldn't explain. Her body was perfect with clothes—without, she was a vision to behold. Even hidden behind the leather mask, her eyes glinted with intrigue. They were the most captivating green I'd ever seen, locking me in place, like a leash had been wrapped around my neck. I had no doubt being this up close and personal that she was wearing a wig, but the fake red locks gave her a sexy fucking vibe that was hard to ignore.

"Do as you please with me, Sir."

Her soft voice broke me from my trance, snapping me back to the present. Stepping forward, I gripped her chin, forcing her to look up at me.

"Your body will belong to me after tonight. Are you prepared to submit yourself to me and only to me?"

She held my gaze, searching my eyes for what I wasn't sure. Everything about her had me feeling on edge—which was unusual for me. She might not know it yet, but this woman may very well hold the power that would be my undoing.

My cock pressed against the leather, begging to be let loose of the confines. I needed to know she was willing to belong to me—even if it was only for tonight.

Like a rubber band being stretched to its breaking point, I snapped when she spoke the one word it took to release the monster, pleading to be let out.

"*Yes.*"

two

RILEY

MY MIND WANDERED to my night at Fantasia, making me heat with excitement. I took a risk joining the club, but I needed to let that part of me out, or it would interfere with my whole reason for being in Vegas. My blood burned as I recalled the way he commanded my body. He didn't know who I was, but I knew everything about him.

Vincenzo Anastasi.

It was a shock seeing him at Fantasia when he sat down next to me at the bar. For a second, I was paralyzed with fear he'd recognize me. His family, the Mafia, controlled Vegas. They owned the club, the restaurant I was working at, and the construction company his brother owned. It gave them more power than anyone. But Vincenzo… he screamed something other than power. He screamed *danger*.

Danger I should've avoided but didn't. And now, I couldn't stop thinking about him, even though I knew it was wrong. If he knew it was me at the club *or* who I really was, he'd have my head removed from my body. Stripping my clothes off, I stepped beneath the warm spray of my shower. I had to push the thoughts of my night tied to the bedposts at his mercy deep into the recess of my mind and step into the version of me everyone else thought they knew.

My need to be dominated in the bedroom was a part of me I kept hidden. In my line of work, I needed to command respect. If my coworkers knew what I did in the dark, they would no longer show me the reverence I needed to run a kitchen.

Stepping out of the shower, I dried off and wiped away the fog covering the glass on my mirror. Staring at the reflection looking back at me, I wondered how I managed to pull off living two lives this long. My hair hung against my skin as the water dripped down my back. As I brushed through the tangled locks, my mind raced with today's events.

I was working at Bellissimo as an assistant to the head chef. I trained as a sous-chef in another lifetime, a life I often pushed from my mind—one filled with pain I preferred not to remember. It was a hell of a lot easier to keep it buried than face the evil that tainted my past. I closed my eyes as the memories washed over me.

"What do you mean, he's dead?" I paced the hallway of the emergency room.

"We're sorry, ma'am. The wounds he sustained were grave. We couldn't do anything to help him."

"This can't be right, please. My father can't be dead."

The doctor placed his hand on my shoulder. "The police would like to speak with you when you're ready."

"Fine."

I shook the vision from my mind. It was the last thing I needed clouding my judgment right now. Today, I needed to embody the part of me that would allow perfection if I was going to play the part of a chef. Quickly pulling my blonde hair into a tight braid, I hurried to finish getting ready. Glancing at the clock, I noticed I needed to step it up, or I was going to be late. I pulled on a pair of black pants and a white blouse that matched the black heels on my feet, giving me a sophisticated look. One I hoped would give me an edge.

Opening my closet, I let my hand graze the white jacket that held my past's pain. It had been a gift from my father when I graduated from culinary school. He'd been so proud that day, watching as I slipped on the embroidered coat for the first time. Inhaling a deep breath, I pulled the jacket from the hanger and slipped it on. Feelings of uncertainty plagued me as I fastened the buttons.

I grabbed my keys, slipped my phone into my pocket, and hurried out the door. My new apartment was close enough I could walk to the restaurant. The streets of Vegas were already alive as I stepped onto the pavement. Sounds of the casinos wafted through the air, mixing with the scent of stale cigars and alcohol.

Crossing the road, I hurried inside. I was pushing against the clock and wanted to be on time. Stepping into the nearly empty restaurant, my eyes searched, looking for something—no, someone.

"I see you've graced me with your presence early." His mocking tone rubbed me wrong, as if he intentionally tried to get under my skin.

"Fuck off, Vincenzo. I always *come* on time." I realized how loaded my words were when he tensed.

A moment of lust flashed in his eyes before he schooled his expression.

"Yes. It would seem you do. Now…" He turned and headed into the kitchen. "We have a lot of prep work to do, and I may need to leave. I'm awaiting word on my brother. As you know, he was involved in an accident while on vacation."

I hurried behind him, keeping my distance. Even in the kitchen, he commanded the room and was not someone to trifle with.

"How is he, your brother?"

"Alive." Vincenzo let his guard down for a moment, allowing me to see a softer side of him.

"Good. If you need anything, let me help. That's why you hired me."

His cellphone vibrated in his pocket. "Excuse me, I need to take this."

He turned his back to me and slipped the phone out. I tried not to eavesdrop, but he didn't make any attempts to be quiet when he spoke.

"Vincenzo." He barked into the line. His brow raised in surprise as I moved toward him. "Yes. Give me a few moments to finish up with Riley and I'll meet you there." He turned and smiled. "I'm sorry. I need to go in a moment."

"No worries. I'll take care of everything. I hope everything is okay with your brother."

"My brother?" He glanced at me, seemingly perplexed.

"Earlier, you said you were waiting for word about your brother. I assume that's what the call was about."

"Oh. Yes. Can you handle this?" He motioned to the prep table.

"Of course, Vincenzo," I assured, rolling my eyes at him.

He held my gaze, silently at war with himself, before finally relenting to whatever it was he was thinking.

"Call if something comes up."

I watched as he turned and left the kitchen. Something big was going on with his brother. What, I had no idea. In time, I hoped I'd get him to open up to me, but until then, I would have to be patient. I needed him to trust me. Everything depended on having his trust, so I wasn't going to push it and risk fucking up my chance.

Turning to the copious amounts of vegetables strewn across the prep table, I pushed thoughts of his disappearance from my head and got to work.

With Vincenzo, I knew to earn his trust, I'd have to ensure his prized possession, the restaurant, was seen to and taken care of. Otherwise, he'd fire me on the spot—defeating my whole reason for existing in this place.

Him.

three

VINCENZO

THE HOUSE WAS a measure of the man's over-inflated ego—an ego that would eventually be his downfall if I had anything to do with it.

"It's empty." I called out as I stepped out of the monstrosity Dmitri called home.

"Where is he?" Bastian growled in frustration, kicked his foot into the dirt.

"I don't know, but Katya was definitely here. I found where she was being held."

"Show me." Matias pushed past me and started up the steps, but I hurried to intercept him.

"Wait, Matias." I jogged up behind him and grabbed his arm. "You need to know there is evidence of…" My voice trailed off, trying to find a delicate way of putting what I had seen.

"Evidence of what?" He snapped, jerking free of my grasp.

"Look. I don't think her stay here has been all that pleasant."

He burst through the front door and raced up the stairs, leaving me outside with his brother.

"You should follow him. What he's about to walk into is going to cause him a great deal of pain."

He nodded and took off up the stairs. I stood with my arms folded and waited for what I knew was to come. When I heard Matais' roar of pain, I knew he'd seen exactly what I'd found. He was a sick man to allow his daughter to be harmed, like the evidence indicated she had been.

My phone rang, startling me to the present. "Vincenzo." I barked into the device.

"Tell Massimo we will meet you at Bellissimo. We will do what we can to help bring this monster in." Miguel's deep voice filled the line before it was gone.

Glancing at the blank screen, sounds of footsteps alerted me to the others' presence. I glanced up and found my brother watching me.

"Miguel is going to meet us at Bellissimo. He'll help us search the locations."

Massimo nodded in approval. "The more we have helping, the faster we'll locate her." He strode toward his SUV and got in, motioning for the others.

Matias climbed into the backseat and slammed the door. I knew he was at war with himself right now. He felt power-less, and that scared him—a feeling I knew all too well. The only way I could have any sense of control was at Fantasia.

My dick pulsed beneath my zipper as thoughts of the redhead filled my mind. Something about her eased the darkness inside me, and I knew one night with her hadn't been nearly enough for me. I wanted—*needed*—to make her my submissive permanently if she agreed to my request.

I straddled my bike and tore off. I knew Miguel would prove to be an asset to us. Having his men assist in finding Dmitri's location, or at least where he was holding Katya, would reduce the time spent looking. After the short ride into Vegas, I pulled into the parking lot. The others had already arrived and were seated in a private room at the back of Bellissimo.

"Hey, Boss." Riley smiled at me as I entered. "Your party is waiting for you."

"Great." Forcing a smile on my face, I nodded toward her. "Make sure we aren't disturbed."

"Sure thing. Do you need me to bring you anything? Drinks or food?"

"Drinks would be good. Thanks, Riley."

Miguel was seated at the table with Matias, Bastian, Massimo, and Donny.

"Vincenzo, I was catching Miguel up. From what we've learned, Ivanov has multiple warehouses around Vegas. Miguel's agreed to have his men start searching them while we try to pinpoint Dmitri's location."

"What do you want me to do?" I sat down and waved Riley into the room. "Everyone, this is my manager, Riley."

"Hello." She smiled as she handed out drinks to the guys openly ogling her. I let out a low growl without realizing it, causing her to shoot me a shocked glare.

"If you need anything else, let me know. I'll leave you alone and make sure no one disturbs you."

"Thanks." I watched as she walked out, my eyes trailing her backside. It was the first time I really noticed how beautiful she was.

Bastian chuckled, drawing my attention to him.

"Your manager is a real looker."

"She's off limits," I grunted, shocked at the possessiveness that burst to the surface. "She knows nothing about this part of the business and for now, we need to keep it that way."

"My apologies. I meant no disrespect." Bastian held his hand up. "I only meant she is a beautiful woman."

"Sorry I snapped." Letting out a frustrated breath, I shook my head. "I am a bit on edge. Dmitri has attacked our family multiple times. I want his head on a spike."

"Trust me, we understand. That's why this alliance has come at a good time." Matias patted Bastian's back. "Let us come up with a plan. I want his head as much as you do… but first, I need to find Katya."

We continued our conversation and planned how we would hunt him down. We would work the locals here in Vegas, while Miguel handled searching the warehouses. Bidding everyone farewell, I found Riley in the back office.

"Everything okay with your family?" Her genuine concern tugged at my heart.

"Yes. Nothing you need to be concerned with." I stepped around her and picked up a towel. "How are things here? I know I've been absent, but you can tell me if there are any issues."

"Everything is wonderful. You have a fantastic staff and system in place. I don't have to do much." She shrugged, brushing off my concern.

"You don't give yourself enough credit, Riley. My absence would have a negative impact on the staff if you weren't here to keep things running. So, thank you for that." I tossed the dish rag onto the counter and leaned against it. "Tell me about you. I feel like I haven't taken the time to get to know you."

She fidgeted nervously. "What do you mean?"

"I know your references had a lot to say about you, but beyond your resume, I don't really know you. Tell me what you do outside of being a chef."

"I'm afraid I'm boring. I work, go home, then do it all again the next day. I don't have time for anything else."

"That does sound boring. Surely a beautiful woman as yourself makes time for more… pleasurable things." I noticed the at my words.

"No, I'm afraid not." A blush crept up her neck as she ran her fingers through her hair, making me wonder why she was lying.

"You shouldn't deny yourself a little fun. Vegas is the city that never sleeps. Go out, enjoy what the city has to offer."

"Is that what you do? Enjoy yourself?"

My cock hardened at her question. If only she knew the depravity I partook in, she would run from this room.

"When I can, yes. Everyone needs a little excitement in their life. Be sure to take advantage of that before you run out of time. We don't know what tomorrow brings." I turned to walk out before pausing in the hallway. "Life is full of choices. Sometimes we make good ones, sometimes we make bad ones. The ones we make in between are what fill us with purpose. Go find your purpose, Riley. You're too young to live such a dull life."

RILEY

I SAT AT MY DESK, surfing through information about the Anastasi family. My phone vibrated beside me on the table, drawing my attention from the computer. Glancing, I unlocked the screen and groaned when I saw who it was.

How's the job?

Rolling my eyes, I typed out my response.

Going as expected. Anything new on your end?

I went back to sifting through the photos of the family online. Vincenzo was even more handsome in person, and the pictures I'd found didn't do him any justice. My phone bounced across the surface of the desk, alerting me to another text.

No. Nothing to report here. I'll check in again in a few days. Good luck.

I sent a quick response and tossed the phone aside. Closing the laptop, I stood. I was feeling restless and needed to release some pent-up energy before going to work. Noting the time, I decided to visit Fantasia again. It was one of the first places I sought when I moved to Vegas. At first, I was afraid to risk joining the club, knowing who owned the place, but I knew privacy was of the utmost concern at Fantasia, so I took the chance I'd stay unknown.

My carnal desires needed an outlet, and it provided me the sanctuary to do so without the fear of being found out. When Vincenzo asked what I did for pleasure, I wanted to tell him he already knew, but keeping my identity secret was paramount for many reasons.

Stripping, I pulled on a new corset and thigh-high stockings. The crotchless panties I slipped into made me feel empowered. I tugged a fitted dress over the black satin and lace, covering the naughty lingerie. The last touch was the red wig that hid my blonde locks, preventing anyone from recognizing me. Tonight, I needed to give myself to someone who would command my body and make me forget my responsibilities… just for a little while.

The cab took me to the place I'd fantasized all day—Fantasia. I pushed through the throngs of people and pressed my keycard to the elevator panel. A small part of me hoped I would find the man I should be avoiding upstairs, but I didn't get my hopes up. I'd be happy with any willing Dom tonight. The room was lively when I stepped off the elevator and handed my coat off to the girl behind the desk. Several sets of eyes tracked my movement as I made my way to the bar and took a seat. I hoped someone worthy would seek my company and take control of both our pleasures. It didn't take long for my wish to come true.

The atmosphere stilled as he walked into the main room, and my breath caught in my throat when our eyes connected. I couldn't control my body's reaction just from seeing him stalk across the floor toward me. His smile caught me off guard, causing the blush to deepen across my pale skin. The nearness of his body had my pulse humming like a live wire. I was positive the thump of my heart could be heard by everyone in the room who were watching us with apt attention.

Leaning onto my side, his lips brushed the soft flesh beneath my ear.

"Hello, Red. Are you in the mood to play?"

"Yes."

My breath caught with excitement as he guided me off the stool and held my hand in his. I wasn't blind to the looks we were getting. It was a powerful feeling to be his for the night.

"I've been looking for you, Red. Where have you been?"

"Around. I've been busy, Sir."

He sucked his teeth, pausing to look back at me.

"That won't do. You need to make time for a little fun in your life. A beautiful woman like you deserves to be tied to a bed." He ran his hand down my arm and leaned into my side as he whispered, "Follow me."

I held onto his hand as he navigated us through the masses of people toward the back. Stepping inside the room, he pressed the door closed and stripped off his shirt.

"Remove your clothes and kneel," he commanded.

My body complied out of need as I shed my clothing, leaving me in the corset I'd dawned before coming here. Dropping to the ground, I bowed my head and waited.

"I am your master tonight." He walked around me, running his hand across my bare shoulders. "You will do as I say. Do you understand?"

"Yes, Sir."

"Good. Stand."

I pushed to my feet and waited. His hand wrapped around my waist and untied the ribbon holding the corset against my skin. As soon as it dropped to the floor, his hands sought my breast. His fingers pinched the tender flesh of my nipple, eliciting a moan from my lips. My pussy pulsed with need, aching to be touched.

"Do you like that?" He squeezed again, his other hand drifting between my legs. "Answer me."

"Yes. I like it."

His fingers dipped between the pink flesh, pressing inside of me as he bit my neck. I thrashed against him, willing him to fuck me without words. He walked us to the bed and tossed me down.

"Roll over."

Moving to my back, I spread my legs in invitation. I watched through the slits of my mask as he eased down his pants. His cock sprang free—angry, red, and swollen.

"Take me in your mouth."

He stepped to the edge of the bed, beckoning me closer. I sat up and crawled my way to the edge of the mattress and gripped him. He grunted as his hips thrust forward, causing the head of his dick to brush against my cheek. I turned my face and took him in my mouth. His groans of approval fueled my desire. His hand instinctively went to my hair, fisting it. I paused, speaking around his shaft.

"Easy. I want to remain anonymous. Please don't pull off my wig."

He let go of my wig. "Then perhaps we should change positions. Get back on the bed."

I released his cock with an audible pop and climbed backward on the bed. He moved around me, securing my arms and legs in binds. I watched in amazement as he opened a drawer and removed a flogger. He dragged the wand across my belly, causing me to shiver beneath the cool leather. I hissed as he slapped it against my skin. A shiver ransacked my body as he toyed with the crotchless panties.

"Did you wear these for me?"

"Yes." I watched him beneath my hooded gaze.

Smiling, he pressed his knee into the mattress between my legs. His fingers thrust into me as he paddled my clit with the flogger. I was so close to release, but my body was fighting it. Sensing my struggle, he pulled his digits from my channel and slid from the bed. He quickly sheathed himself in a condom and took position above me.

"I know what you need, Red." He rammed his cock inside me, forcing my body against the bed. He rocked into me as he gripped the headboard. "I will own your body. Feel my dick as it moves inside you. Tell me, Red. Tell me I own your body."

"Yes," I moaned, thrashing as he destroyed my pussy for all others. "You own me… please don't stop." I was begging him to push me over the edge of bliss. He picked up the pace, giving into my wish with each thrust of his hips.

"Please, Sir," I whimpered as my body began to tighten around him.

He pulled out, releasing my binds, and flipped me to my stomach. Arching my ass, he smacked his palm against the tender flesh and shoved inside me again. His movements were relentless as he pounded into my pussy. I could feel the tingling building as he drove us both closer to the edge. I teetered there, ready to jump off the cliff with him.

"I can't hold out much longer. I need you to come, Red."

My body reacted, clamping down around his shaft. My juices flooded out, coating his cock in my desire. He bellowed out as his orgasm broke free. Gripping my hips, he was driving in and out, grunting behind me as his cum spilled inside the condom. He rolled off me, shed the condom, and tossed it into a nearby trashcan.

I adjusted my mask, ensuring it was secured to my face as I stood up from the bed. Gathering my dress from the floor, I cleaned myself up and tugged it over my head.

"I want you again, Red. Where are you running off to? The night is young."

"I need to get some sleep." I smiled. "Some of us have to work."

"I'm sure your boss would understand if you took a day off."

"You don't know my boss. He's a ruthless man and doesn't take kindly to incompetent workers." I smiled, knowing he was the boss.

"Sounds like a real prick."

I couldn't contain the giggle that burst from my lips. "If you only knew."

"Can we make this a regular thing, perhaps?"

"What do you mean?" I tugged on my heels and paused with my hand on the doorknob.

He stepped behind me and pressed his chest into my back.

"Be my sub. Let me command your body here at Fantasia. We can meet here often and work out our frustrations from our daily lives."

Leaning into his hardened muscles, I inhaled his scent. His cock was already standing at attention as he pressed against my ass. Everything in me said to walk out the door, but I couldn't. I wanted to be his too much—damn the consequences. If I kept my identity a secret, he couldn't hurt me, and I couldn't hurt him.

"Fine. I get off at midnight most nights. I'll come here to find you."

He grasped my chin and forced my head back. His lips claimed mine in a possessive kiss that left my insides burning with passion. Slipping from his grasp, I darted out the door and ran to the elevator. I'd just agreed to be the Devil's mistress. I should feel regret or shame… but all I felt was desire.

What *had* I done?

five

VINCENZO

I STOOD with my back against the wall, watching as Riley commanded the kitchen. She had proven to be a good fit here at Bellissimo. I laughed as she dropped a bowl on the floor, swearing out loud as she did.

"Calm down, Tesoro." I picked the metal bowl up and tossed it into the sink. "I think you need a break."

"No, I'm fine." She wiped her brow with the back of her hand, smearing sauce across her forehead.

"You're making a mess of yourself." I pulled the towel out from my back pocket and brushed it across her skin, wiping away the dribble of liquid on her face.

She grabbed the towel from my hand and continued to clean herself up.

"Thanks."

"Seriously, Riley. You need a break. What is it you like to do when you're not here?"

"Why are you so worried about my private life, Vin? What about yours? Where do you go every time the phone rings? When you return, you're even more stressed than when you left." She snapped, throwing the towel onto the counter.

She wasn't wrong. I left angry and returned even angrier.

"My family is working through some things."

"Maybe it's you who needs a woman."

I laughed at her candor with me. "I don't have time for relationships."

"Hogwash. I didn't say girlfriend. I said a woman. You know one for your carnal needs."

I stepped closer to her, crowding her against the edge of the counter.

"Someone for fucking?" I was blunt with my words, making her squirm.

"I…" she stuttered. "Yes. That's what I meant."

"Are you offering?"

"What?" she gasped, pretending to be offended, but the way her nipples pebbled beneath her chef's jacket, I knew she was lying. "No. You're my boss."

"I'm kidding." Stepping back, I placed some space between us. "Besides, I'm partial to redheads." I saw a flicker of something cross her face, but she turned away.

"Oh. Well, good thing I'm not a redhead." She stepped around me, heading for the door. "If you don't need me, I think I'll go home for the night."

"You should go out, live a little." I flicked the light off and walked behind her toward the back door. "If you want, you could go to my brother's club and have a fun time. I'll call him and let him know you're coming."

"Discoteca?"

"Yep. Go. Have a drink on me."

"Maybe I will." She walked toward her apartment. "What will you do tonight, Vincenzo?"

"I have some things to attend to with Antonio."

"Oh." Her voice deflated with disappointment, surprising me.

Quirking my lips into a tiny grin, I nodded toward her as I locked the restaurant.

"I'll see you tomorrow evening, Riley." I climbed onto my bike and watched as she disappeared around the corner.

Antonio was waiting for me at the warehouse. Another one of Dmitri's men had been nabbed, and they were trying to get information out of him. He was refusing to speak, but once I got there, he would risk his life for his silence.

The ride to Antonio's was refreshing. The cool air kissed my skin as the lights of Vegas lit my path. Being on my bike was one of the few other times I felt in control of my life. The other was when I was fucking a woman at Fantasia.

I navigated the bike through the gates of our family's construction yard. We had several warehouses, mainly for lumber storage, but the one I parked in front of was the farthest away from the main strip. It allowed for more privacy when we needed to exert a paltry force on those trying to hurt our family.

Antonio was leaning against the wall when I entered the open space. A man, already sporting the beating I was certain Donny had given him, sat strapped to a chair.

"Vincenzo. Glad to see you made it to the party."

The man's eyes widened with recognition when he spied me at the entrance.

"I wouldn't miss this opportunity." I slipped out the blade hidden in my boot and spun it between my fingers. The cool metal ignited the darkness in my blood, begging to be set free. "Are you ready to tell us what we need to know?"

"I cannot betray the Prizrak." He spoke in a deep Russian accent. "Death is an honor, and I'll die protecting him."

"Have it your way." I nodded to Antonio and Donny, signaling to them I was about to begin. I gripped the man by his head, tilting it back. "Are you sure the pain I'm about to inflict on you is worth protecting him?"

"Fuck you," he rasped out as his beady eyes narrowed on me.

"You'll burn in Hell for this." I pressed the blade against his skin. "Don't be a martyr. Give us what we want."

"No. I'll die a thousand deaths before I betray him."

"You're willing to die a thousand deaths for nothing. When I'm done with you, you will feel as though you have done just that."

Running the blade down his jaw, I sliced a thin line into his flesh. Blood trickled along the silver of the knife as the edge filleted his face. He cried out in pain, jerking against the restraints as I leaned into him.

"Last chance before the blade removes your tongue."

He flinched against my grasp but made no attempt to answer our questions. Inhaling a deep breath, I closed my eyes and gave into the darkness. His screams filled the warehouse as I let my blade dance along his body.

The black void consumed me as I stared at the blood covering my hands. The man lying on the concrete was one of many who had died at these hands over the last couple of weeks. After Antonio had been kidnapped by Dmitri, the part of me I worked so hard to bury emerged with a need for vengeance. The metallic scent in the air confirmed there was no going back to normal.

"Damn, Brother." Antonio peered over my shoulder at the mutilated body at my feet. "You really did a number on him."

"He didn't have any information. Have Donny dump his body on Dmitri's property. He may not be there, but someone will tell him. I want him to know La Lama is after him. He did this when he came after the family. Trying to frame me for Miguel's sister's death was only the beginning. Then what they did to Catarina, you, and now Katya…" I blew out a breath as I rubbed the bridge of my nose.

"Catarina and I are both okay. Don't let the need for retaliation consume you, Vin."

I stiffened beside him. "The moment we had to dig into my past, Pandora's box was opened, Antonio. The need to control and inflict pain is too much."

"Visit the club. Go hunting… for animals. But this,"— Antonio waved toward the carnage— "isn't you… not anymore."

"You're wrong. It's always been me." I left Antonio standing in front of the warehouse and headed toward my bike.

I always carried hand wipes and a shirt in the backpack strapped to the seat in case I had to get my hands dirty. The blood stained the white cotton, turning it a deep shade of pink as I rubbed away the evidence from my hands. I stripped off the carnage-stained shirt and pulled on the clean one. Shoving the wadded-up wipe and stained shirt into the bag, I tugged on my helmet and straddled my bike.

The rev of the engine rattled my bones. The power beneath me grounded me in ways I sought after I fell into the obscurity of death. Antonio was right. I was teetering on the edge of being lost to my past all over again. La Lama, a nickname I earned for all the bloodshed and destruction I left in my wake when I was younger, was blossoming again.

My father knew if he needed someone eliminated, I was the person who could get in and out. They called what I did with my blade an art. I called it the Devil's handiwork. I still felt the need to dominate, to feel someone beg for mercy. As I pulled out on the main road, my bike had a mind of its own and headed in the one direction I could hear pleas of mercy without murder on my hands.

Parking my bike behind Discoteca, I slipped my leg over the seat and unstrapped my bag. Walking past the bouncer, I let myself in ahead of the crowd gathering at the door. No one dared to say anything to me since they all knew who I was. Massimo was leaning against the bar, his hand resting against Madison's hip. They glanced in my direction and nodded. I didn't feel like talking to anyone. I was on the edge of losing it, so I dipped my head and headed to the elevators. What I needed was on the second floor. There, I could let the demon out and not be scrutinized. I dug the key card out, pressed it to the sensor, and waited.

"Vin." Massimo stepped behind me.

"Not now, Massimo," I growled, not looking in his direction.

"I'm worried about you. Antonio called me. He told me what happened."

"And? You both knew what would happen if we ventured into my past. A past I begged you to leave alone."

He blew out a frustrated breath. "I didn't think you would fall into that life again, Vincenzo."

"You didn't think a part of my life I worked hard to bury would rear its ugly head when I was forced to become that again?"

"No. You're not him anymore."

"That's where you're wrong, Fratello." I finally turned toward him, pinning him with a glare. "La Lama is and always will be a part of me. Burying him was never meant to be permanent. I just thought he would stay buried longer. But we resurrected the Devil thanks to Dmitri, and now…" I stepped into the elevator and turned to look at him. "Dmitri will get what he wanted. La Lama will come for him and *destroy* him."

The doors closed, leaving Massimo stunned on the other side. I hated to be so blunt, but it was the truth. There would be no peace for anyone as long as the darkness was streaming through my veins. Until my knife was slipping through the soft flesh of Dmitri's neck, La Lama would stay risen.

six

RILEY

"Do you have any information yet?" Jackson's brooding voice filled the line.

"Nope. He's very private and is not amicable when trying to get him to open up." The truth was, I hadn't been trying hard to get close to Vincenzo.

"Riley, you've been on the job for over a month. How is it you have nothing yet?"

"You're right. I've been at it for a little over a month. That's hardly enough time to earn his trust. You knew this would take time, Jackson." I huffed in frustration.

"Fine. Find me something, Riley, and soon, or Pritz is going to pull you off this assignment."

"There is no need for that. Give me more time. I'll get the information we need. I promise."

"Time is of the essence, Riley." Jackson's irritated tone did not go unnoticed. "It's the only way we can bring them down."

I agreed to up my game and disconnected the call. Tossing my phone into my bag, I pressed my hands to my face and screamed. My body craved control—the control I had been getting at the hands of the very man I shouldn't be. Guilt plagued me as I rode in the cab toward Fantasia.

How had I made such a mess of my life? I was only supposed to gain his trust and find information that would give the FBI evidence they needed to link him to La Lama—one of the two hitmen we knew the mob used. For the last eight years he avoided… rather evaded authorities. La Lama was as sought after as the Prizrak, Dmitri Ivanov. Neither of who I was any closer to finding.

Climbing from the confines of the cab, I quickly headed toward the club. I needed to give over my control. Truthfully, what I needed was to be commanded by *his* touch. I knew he would be there. Once he knew I would show up after midnight, he was always there waiting.

Just as I suspected, he was sitting at the bar when I arrived on the second floor. I followed him into the playroom, stripped naked, and dropped to my knees. Vincenzo ran his hand along my bare back as he prowled around me.

"Good girl." He paused in front of me. "Now take off my pants and show me how much you desire me."

I reached up and eased the zipper of his leather pants down. My heart raced with a beat that rivaled even the fastest horse. Everything about this was wicked. I should've walked out the door and not looked back. Instead, I hauled him free of his pants, his cock pleading for my touch as it pulsated against my palm.

My core quaked with need as I slipped his bulbous head into my mouth. The salty taste of his pre-cum battered my taste buds as I swallowed him deeper. His moans only fueled my yearning as I moved against him. My body inundated with need as I sucked him off.

"Stop." He drew away, his cock slipping from between my lips. "Stand," he ordered as he backed away from my spot on the floor.

I stood and waited for his orders. My body was burning with want as I watched him sheath himself in a condom and stride toward me.

"I need to punish you tonight, Red. Can you handle the pain?"

My pussy pulsed with need, thinking about him spanking me.

"Yes."

"Lay on the bench, ass up."

He pointed to the wooden bench in the middle of the room. Moving swiftly, I laid my body across the smooth surface and waited for his castigation.

"What's your safe word, Red?"

"Purple."

"Good. Use it if this becomes too much, but I need this as much as I suspect you do."

"I will." I nodded as the excitement bubbled in my chest. "Please, Sir. I need this."

The first lash stung my flesh, sending tiny tendrils of pain straight to my core. My pussy pulsated with desire as he struck me again. Each time the leather grazed my skin, my body flooded with exhilaration. With each strike of the strap, his hand soothed the tender flesh.

"Are you all right?"

"Yes." I half-whispered, half-moaned.

"One last time, then I will give you the pleasure you've earned." The leather came down against my skin one last time, as promised, causing me to cry out in ecstasy. He dropped the strip of cowhide and gripped my hips. His fingers dug into me as he pushed inside me, burying himself to the hilt.

"Fuck," he grunted against me as his dick throbbed with need.

"Please, Sir. I need you to move," I begged, widening my gait. My body demanded release—one that was close to the surface.

He withdrew and thrust into me with unrelenting force. His nails bit into my skin as he pounded into my center. He was mad with need, nearly as mad as I was. My body rubbed against the wooden edge of the bench as his cock drove in and out of my channel. The sensations of his hands on my skin and the friction of oak against my swollen clit had me toppling over into the abyss. My body clenched around his shaft, forcing him over with me. He groaned loudly, rutting behind me as his cock swelled and ruptured inside me. I saw stars as the orgasm ripped from my body. Vincenzo dropped to his knees, his dick slipping out of me as he laid across my back, panting against my skin.

"Jesus Christ."

I breathed into the room, completely stunned by what I'd just experienced.

"What was that?"

"That was me claiming you, Red. After tonight, you're *mine*."

Wiggling beneath him, I pushed him off. "Move. I need to leave."

His head jerked up at my hasty exit. "Why are you running?"

"I can't be yours." I gathered my clothes and pulled them on as best as I could. "This shouldn't have happened. I'm sorry."

Leaving the room, I stopped to grab my coat. When I emerged from the coatroom, Vincenzo was leaning against the wall with nothing but his pants on. He shook his head as I pressed my keycard to the panel.

"You're wrong, Red. We're good together. Just tell me who you are, and we can make this something more."

My eyes glistened with tears as I held his gaze.

"This is all it can be." I disappeared into the elevator and leaned against the metal wall.

What had I done?

Years of planning and one night was threatening to destroy everything I'd worked for. I couldn't let what was happening between the version of me that wasn't real… steer me off course. I would go to work and pretend this was all a bad dream. Even as I thought it, I knew it wouldn't be possible.

I knew I was no longer risking my career.

No… this time, my heart was at risk—and that scared the ever-loving shit out of me.

seven

VINCENZO

"BROTHER, ARE YOU WITH US?" Massimo's voice cut through my thoughts. My mind was still at the club with Red.

"Yes, sorry. What did you say?"

Antonio's laughter made me blush, reminding me I needed to focus on the matter at hand.

"Massimo, it would appear our brother has been bewitched by a woman. Who is she, Vin?" he probed, knowing damn well he was right.

"What?" Ignoring his correct assumption, I rolled my eyes and blew him off. "No, you're wrong. There is no woman."

"Are you sure? It wouldn't be a bad thing, Vin. A woman could help keep your mind occupied." Massimo tossed a pen to the table. "I've been worried you're in too deep with the search for Dmitri."

"We have to find him. My involvement is necessary, and you know it." Massimo's grunt of disapproval filled the room at my insistence of getting involved.

"I do. That doesn't mean I can't worry about you. You worked hard to bury that part of you, the part you hated when we were younger. And now…" Massimo sighed. "You've fallen right back into being him—La Lama. What happens when that version of you takes over completely, and I lose you again… this time forever?"

"You won't lose me. Once Dmitri is dead, I will go back to being me, the famous chef."

"I still think finding a woman would do you some good." Antonio pressed his hand against my shoulder. "Look at how much it's helped, Massimo. He's not nearly as much of a dick as he was."

"He's not wrong." Massimo shrugged, proving once again Antonio was right. "Madison has softened me—something I desperately needed. *Something* you desperately need."

"Can we stop talking about my love life, or lack thereof, and focus on the problem?"

"Right. Dmitri was spotted at the airport, but our men lost sight of him. The important thing is we know he is here. Miguel has assured me his men are keeping a close watch on his property and warehouses. If he shows up, we will know."

"Why is he here in Vegas?" Antonio began to pace the room behind me. "It seems dangerous for him to come back now."

"Can you sit down?" I quirked my brow at him. "Your pacing is annoying the shit out of me." My phone vibrated in my pocket, causing me to jerk. Slipping my hand inside, I pulled it out, shocked to see Riley calling. Holding my finger up to quiet my brothers, I pressed the speaker button.

"Vincenzo."

"Vin." Her panicked voice filled the line. I could hear the urgency in her tone, causing me to sit up straighter in my chair.

"Riley. What's wrong?"

"I know you're busy, but one of the servers is missing and I don't know what to do."

"What do you mean, missing?" I relaxed slightly, figuring one whoever it was messed up their work schedule.

"Megan didn't show up for work. I've tried calling her with no luck."

"Maybe she's just sick or got her days mixed up."

"I thought that, too, but then a note came by courier. You need to see this, Vin."

Massimo stood and waved toward Antonio as I stood.

"Sit tight, Riley. My brothers and I are on the way to you."

"Should I call the police?"

"No. Wait for me to get there first." I pressed the end button and shoved the phone into my pants. "Dmitri is behind this."

"I have no doubt, Brother. Let's go. If he has Megan, we need to find her before it's too late." The three of us exited out of the club into the alley.

Donny was waiting in the car. Massimo and Antonio climbed inside as I straddled my bike. Following behind them, my mind raced with a million thoughts. Why was Dmitri back, and what was his end game?

I parked my bike and hurried inside to find Riley seated at a table. Her expression was weary and filled with concern.

"Riley!" I called, causing her to stand abruptly.

"Vincenzo." She thrust the letter at me and watched as I opened it.

Rage coursed through me as I read the words scratched into the parchment.

You may have won round one, but you have only angered the Prizrak. I'm coming for you and your family… not even La Lama can protect you. This is just the beginning of my hold over you. Everyone and everything close to you… will die.

"What does it mean by La Lama can't protect you? Vincenzo?"

"Brother." Antonio pulled the letter from my fist, nearly ripping it in two. "Sit down."

"We need to call the police." Riley started around the table, but Massimo grabbed her by the arm.

"No. We can't involve them. Sit down, Riley. *Please.*"

Riley plopped into a chair, tears rolling down her face. "I don't understand."

"Riley…" Massimo sighed. "I'll explain it all. Just give Vin a chance to calm down."

I ran my hand over my face, sighing as my eyes closed.

"What are we going to do?"

"Donny is already sending men to look for the courier. Where does Megan live? We need to search her place and see if there is anything leading us to her whereabouts. I think it's safe to assume Dmitri has her."

Riley stood. "I'll go grab her information." We watched as she hurried toward the office.

"You're going to have to bring her in on things, Vincenzo. Can we trust her?"

I stared down the empty hallway in her direction. "I'll talk to her."

"That didn't answer my question. Can she be trusted with the family?"

"I believe so. Alec found nothing on her, and she has given me no reason to believe otherwise. I'll talk to her after you leave."

"Here's her personnel file." Riley handed Massimo the folder and stepped back. "I'll just go."

"No, wait." Standing, I grabbed her wrist and looked at my brothers. "Let me know what you find. I need a moment with Riley." Antonio and Massimo saw themselves out, leaving us alone. "I need to know that I can trust you, Riley."

"What do you mean? Of course, you can trust me, but what does that have to do with what's going on?"

"What I'm about to tell you not only puts you at risk, but it puts my entire family at risk as well. I trust you, Riley... I just need to know you can keep this secret."

eight

RILEY

"Riley, are you listening to me?" Vincenzo tilted his head at me, reminding me he was talking. He'd just told me what I already knew. He was in the mob. Hell, it was the whole reason I dug my chef's coat out of the closet and pretended to be the girl I once had been.

"Hmmm? Yes, I heard you. Your family's secret is safe with me. I'm a loyal employee, Vincenzo. You don't have to worry about me telling anyone I work for the mob."

"Riley, I don't want you to worry. I promise you're safe here."

"It's not that." I paced the floor. "Who is La Lama? Do you know him?"

Vincenzo watched me, his eyes darkening with something sinister. An expression of fear and desire washed through my body.

"Let's not talk about that right now."

"This is serious." I walked toward the office, my mind racing with confusion. "La Lama is one of the most wanted criminals in the world."

"How do you know that?"

"I watch America's Most Wanted." I stuttered, the slip causing him to eye me. "I saw it on there once."

He closed the door to the office, caging me inside the room with him. Vincenzo took several steps toward me, forcing me onto his desk.

"Can I really trust you, Riley?"

"I already told you yes." The sexual tension was profound, making my heart race with uncertainty. His closeness made my insides pulse with need. He leaned into me, and his warm breath caused my pussy to flood with desire.

"I need to be honest with you," he whispered in my ear.

I closed my eyes. "Okay."

"It won't bode well for you if I find out you're keeping anything from me. Do you have any secrets I should know, Riley?" He stepped away, leaving me panting for his touch.

I blinked, realizing what he had said. "No… I told you. You can trust me."

"Good." He walked toward the hallway and turned. "I have to be somewhere. Call me if you need anything. I'll be back in an hour."

I slumped against the wall once he was gone. It felt as if the tiny space was closing in around me, and everything was falling apart at the seams. I needed to gain control of the situation, and fast. Being here was for one purpose and one purpose only—to find evidence Vincenzo knew who La Lama was. The only problem was, I wasn't sure I wanted to find the truth anymore.

My heart and mind were at war with each other, and the worst part was, he didn't even know how I felt. I'd fucked up, and I wasn't sure how to undo my mistakes—or if I even wanted to.

The vibration of my phone startled me. Slipping it from my chef's coat, I pressed it to my ear. "Hello?"

"Meet me at the diner outside of town in thirty." The line when dead, giving me no time to respond.

Glancing at the clock, I huffed. I had two hours before I needed to get the restaurant ready for dinner service. Grabbing my bag, I headed out front and let Kate, the bartender, know I would be back soon. I walked the short distance to my apartment and grabbed my car. This was one headache I didn't need right now.

———

"WHERE ARE YOU ON THE INVESTIGATION?" AGENT Mitchell sat across from me at a diner just outside Vegas.

"I've finally got their trust. Like I said on the phone, this kind of thing takes longer than a few weeks, Mitchell." I was tired of the urgency the bureau was putting on me. A case like this didn't need to be rushed.

"Does he suspect who you are?"

I shrugged. "I don't think so."

"Good. Now, tell me what you've learned. Surely you have something."

"I know the family is having problems with Dmitri Ivanov. He has some vendetta against them."

"Dmitri Ivanov? Holy shit… the Prizrak? Do you know what it could do for your career if you find the Prizrak *and* La Lama? You'll have single-handedly brought down two of the most notorious criminals in the world."

"I have to find them first, and that takes time."

"You can have all the time you need to build this case. I'll let Jackson know you're working a new angle… just don't forget why you're there. You need to tie Vincenzo Anastasi to La Lama. For years he has evaded prosecution. It's time to bust that motherfucker."

"I know." Hearing him say it out loud made my gut churn with unease. "I'm doing my best." The chime over the door echoed through the tiny restaurant, causing me to glance toward the door.

Mitchell was too engrossed in his food to notice one of Vincenzo's men had entered.

"Look, I've got to go. I can't start being late for work now. It'll raise suspicion."

"Alright. You have my number. Call me when you have something."

I tossed a few bills on the table and stood. Taking a deep breath, I walked out the door, conscious of the fact I was being followed. Needing to play dumb, I spun and faced him.

"Look buster." I turned, halting the man in his spot. "I will cut your dick off if you're planning to hurt me."

"Lady,"—his hands went up in defense— "Mr. Anastasi asked me to keep an eye on you. Is there something you're worried about him finding out?"

"No." I turned back to my car and climbed in. "I'm allowed to have lunch with friends." I slammed the car door and screamed. "Fuck." I shoved my keys in the ignition and closed my eyes. If Vincenzo found out who I was meeting with, he would have my head, and years of investigative work would be in the toilet. Life wouldn't matter if my career ended.

Aside from my mother, it was all I had.

nine

SHE WAS HIDING SOMETHING, and it was holding her back. I couldn't put my finger on it, but Riley was harboring a secret that kept her at arm's length. I watched as she worked effortlessly in the kitchen.

"Riley," I called. "I need to see you in my office."

"You wanted to see me?"

"Yes. Come in and shut the door."

"Um." She paused, glancing toward the hallway.

"I'm not going to hurt you, Riley. Shut the goddamn door."

She pulled it closed and took the seat across from me. Her face reddened with embarrassment as she turned her head and looked away.

"I'm sorry. It's just…"

"Just what? Think I called you in here because I want to fuck you?" She gasped, her eyes finding mine. I expect to see anger in them, but what I find has my cock straining against my pants. "You'd be right, Riley, but that's not why I called you in here now. As you know, Megan is still missing. With the risk of something happening to you, I have someone protecting you until we find him. Care to tell me who you were meeting with yesterday?"

"What?" Riley pushed back and stood. "How *dare* you? What I do on my own time is my business."

"Yes. You're right." My gaze travels the length of her body. "But this man kidnapped my brother. He tried to take my sister. If you are here, you're a target. I was doing what I thought was best." The urge to reach across the desk and pull her across the surface is startling. "You didn't answer my question. Who were you meeting with?"

"This is ridiculous." She threw her hands up into the air and paced nervously.

"Just answer the fucking question," I growled angrily.

"Why? I'm just an employee. It has nothing to do with you or your family."

"You're a target, whether you want to be. I need to know if that man you were with is a threat." Moving around my desk quickly, I backed her against the wall. "Riley, you can deny it, but you're hiding something. I've given you space and left you alone, but I meant what I said the other day. If you're keeping something from me, you will not like the consequence."

"Look." Her head tilted, so she was looking me in the eye. "I won't lie to you. This job is important to me, but my private life is just that—private."

"Why are you being so stubborn?" Pressing my palms to the wall, I caged her in, closing the gap between us. "You know I can find out who he was, with or without your honesty."

"I don't understand." Her brows knit together as her head shakes in disbelief.

"I'm a powerful man, Riley. Secrets never stay that way forever."

Riley cocked her head, mulling over my words. "This is nuts."

Without thinking, I brush my knuckles down her jaw. "I want to trust you. No… I need to trust you."

Her breath hitched and her eyes dilated as she held my gaze. "Why is that so important to you?"

"Family is everything to me, Riley. Trust is something sacred to me, and I want to share that with you, but I can't if you continue to hide things from me. It's dangerous for both of us."

"He was an old friend of my father's." She clutched her stomach as she turned her head away. "My mom told him I was here working, and he just wanted to check in with me."

"See. Was that so hard?" I take a step back and pause. An uncontrollable urge to take what I wanted barreling through my system. I pressed my palm against her face. "Riley." Her name came out as a growl before I slammed my mouth over hers.

She stiffened at first, but the moment my tongue brushed against her lip, she let a moan slip and opened for me. There was something familiar about the way our mouths moved in tandem, but before I could question it further, Riley ripped her lips from mine and darted under my arm.

"I should get back to work."

Grabbing her arm before she succeeded in getting out of the office, I halted her steps.

"Trust, Riley, is earned. You'd do best to remember that."

She wrenched her arm from my grasp and disappeared down the hall, leaving me with a thousand questions and a raging hard-on. Despite the kiss clouding my thoughts, I knew Riley lied to my face about who she was seeing—and I needed to know why. Grabbing my phone, I sat down and called Alec. If anyone could find her secret, it was him.

"Alec, I need a favor."

"What's up, Boss?" He was always quick to help us with our requests. Alec was an important part of the family dynamic, and I'd be forever grateful if he came home to us in one piece. Even if he came back differently, Alec would always be our cousin.

"My new manager is hiding something. I need to know what it is. I know you did a background on her, but something's missing."

He mumbled something I didn't quite hear.

"What did you say?"

"Nothing," he sighed. "Sorry. I'll make some calls and see what I can dig up."

"Do me a favor. Keep this between us."

Alec is silent at first, probably wanting to question me more, but he doesn't. "You got it."

I disconnected the call and thought about calling Benito. I wanted to find out where she went when she left here. Whatever she was hiding wouldn't stay buried forever. And after the kiss we shared, it was well past the time to unmask the real Riley Lawson.

My cell phone drew me from thoughts of her as it skittered across my desk. Massimo's face filled the screen.

"What is it?" I barked into the room after putting him on speaker.

"Miguel's men found Katya."

I sat up straighter. "Where?"

"In one of his warehouses. It's bad, brother. What he did to her…" Massimo's voice trailed off. "She's at Antonio's. Catarina is tending to her now. Vincenzo…"

"We'll find him, brother. I promise you that. Ivanov will not meet a quick end. This has gone on too long, and it's time we turned the tables. I'll be there shortly. You need to tell everyone to be ready—I won't be holding back any longer. He wanted La Lama… well, he's about to get him."

ten

RILEY

I WATCHED as people dined blissfully, unaware of the surrounding atrocities. Megan had not been found yet, and the Anastasis had somehow evaded law enforcement, keeping them unaware of her disappearance. In addition, Vincenzo disappeared for several days without explanation. While it allowed me to keep my distance from him after the highly inappropriate—but permanently scorched into my brain kiss we shared—I had a job to do. A job I was slowly starting to hate.

I wondered what he would do if he learned I was Red. Would he push me against the prepping counter and spank me... then fuck me senseless? Or would he put a bullet in my head for the lies I'd spun so intricately?

"Riley."

Vincenzo's voice cut through the thoughts that had my traitorous body burning with desire. My head snapped up to meet his heated gaze.

"Yes, Sir?" I watched as his body momentarily stiffened.

"Lose the formalities." His eyes narrowed on me as he barked his orders. "I need you back here."

I hurried around the bar and pushed into the kitchen. "What do you need?"

"Grab some carrots and start chopping. The line chef just cut himself and is in the bathroom tending to his wound."

I ran my hand across the granite, pausing to pick up a blade. Spinning the handle between my fingers, I spread the veggies across the cutting board in preparation.

"You know how to handle a knife well." Vincenzo watched with longing as I moved the edge across the surface.

"Don't you?" I chuckled and tossed it to the table when I finished.

"You could say that..." He mumbled, turning back to his work.

We worked seamlessly the rest of the night, nearly dead on our feet, when the crowd finally parted. Vincenzo leaned against the counter and watched as I loaded the last of the pots into the dishwasher and turned it on.

"What are your plans for the night, Riley?" he asked as I wiped my hands down and shed my white linen jacket.

"A hot bath and sleep." I yawned, knowing my intentions were no such thing. I hoped to find him at the club as I had been the last few months.

"How about a drink?"

I blinked, unsure if I heard him right. "A drink?"

"Yeah. You know, like a cocktail... with me?"

"Oh, I don't think we should." Even though everything in me wanted to say yes, I had to keep some distance. "I'm exhausted and just want to get some sleep. Maybe another time?"

Vincenzo stepped a breath away from me and fingered a loose strand of hair at my nape. "Another time, but Riley?"

"Yes?" My voice came out far breathier than I wanted.

"You can keep pretending the kiss didn't happen... but I can't." He stepped away and tugged open the door. "I'll see you tomorrow, Riley."

I followed him out, watching as he locked up and got on his bike. Sending a silent prayer to the heavens that he was going to Fantasia. I hurried down the sidewalk to my apartment. I shouldn't be hoping for things so dangerous, but my body needed what only he could give me.

After showering, dawning only a black lace bra and crotchless panties, I slipped on some heels and my jacket. Making sure the wig was securely in place, I stepped out into the night air. The club felt like it was eons away due to the heady desire driving me to a man I *shouldn't* want. Slipping my mask from my pocket, I secured it to my face before anyone noticed my arrival, then headed in the direction of our private room. Relief washed over me to find him sitting in the chair, watching the door like a predator waiting for his prey.

"I hoped you would come." His voice washed over me, drawing out a shiver.

"I needed to see you." I pushed the door closed behind me.

He pushed to his feet and prowled toward me. The wicked glint in his eyes put my body on high alert. It was the way he moved and the way his eyes devoured me like a man starved.

"I see you dressed for me." His fingers pushed the coat off my shoulders, causing it to slide off and drop to the floor. A deep rumble vibrated in his chest, seeing me in only a lace bra and crotchless panties. His fingertips blazed a trail down my side, his mere touch igniting a fire inside me that only he could put out.

"Do you approve?" My eyes were downcast, waiting for his permission to look at him.

"You're the only woman who has me questioning every-thing." He fingered the black strap of my bra, pushing it to the side as his lips descended to my skin. Brushing the red braid over my shoulder, he latched on to my neck, his teeth nipping my flesh. "I wish you would take this off and let me see the real you." The tip of my wig twirled between his fingers.

I moaned under the heat of his mouth, silently wishing for that, too.

"Sir."

"Why do you wear it? We don't need the role play, Red. Are you hiding something?"

"I…" His lips captured mine as his hand pressed into my belly. "Please… *Sir*."

"Please, what?"

"Make me cum."

He spurred into action, spinning me around and lifting me from the floor. Carrying me to the bed, he gently laid me on the mattress. He slid my panties down and tossed them to the floor.

"Use your safe word if this becomes too much."

"Okay."

"Good girl." I watched beneath the edges of my mask as he gathered a few toys from the nearby dresser. He gently bound my arms and legs to each of the bedposts. Clamps were applied to each nipple just before he stuffed a gag into my mouth.

"Let me hear your safe word, Red."

"Pufurl," I mumbled around the ball.

"Good." He ran his hand up my thigh and stopped at my center. "Tonight, is about pleasure and pain becoming one." He walked around the foot of the bed and picked up a wand. The vibrator whirled to life as he ran his palm across my stomach. Climbing onto the bed, he kneeled between my legs and pressed the toy to my thigh, causing me to jerk against the binds that held me in place.

"You like that, don't you?" He held my gaze as he pressed the vibrator against my center. Every nerve came alive as it rubbed against my clit. I thrashed and moaned as the orgasm built. Just as I was about to topple over the edge, he pulled it away, causing my climax to retreat. "You'll come when I say you come."

"Pwease…" My breathless plea fell on deaf ears.

He tossed the wand to the floor and stepped away from the bed.

"I think I'll try something else." He grabbed a leather whip and snapped it through the air. "I want to open your flesh and see your skin pinked. Can you handle this, Red?"

I nodded, the yes coming out muffled, the ball gag restricting my words. My eyes followed his hands as he flicked his wrist. The tip of the whip brushed against my skin, causing me to cry out around the plastic pressing against my teeth. He continued to command the toy in his hand as the sound of leather cracking against my skin filled the room.

Vincenzo was completely lost in his head, unaware that the pleasure had long ceased or that my cries weren't from pleasure. I couldn't take it anymore. My skin felt like it was being torn from my body with each crack of the torture device.

"Pufurl… Pufurl…" I cried out, begging him to stop around the tears pouring out from behind the mask. The whip lashed out one last time, leaving a trail of blood across my backside before he realized I'd called out my safe word.

"Jesus Christ." He swore, tossing the whip to the floor. "Red."

He rushed to my side, freeing my arms and legs as he moved to pull me against him. I tugged the gag from my mouth as the sobs erupted. For the first time with this man, I felt fear.

"Fuck… I'm so sorry." He pressed kisses to my head. "I-I lost myself."

I lay perfectly still, tears flowing freely as Vincenzo assessed the damage to my flesh. He ran his hands gently over the welts along my rib cage and down my legs. He pressed his lips to the torn skin, kissing the marks he left on my body.

"Can you forgive me?" His voice cracked with emotion I didn't expect as he begged for my forgiveness. "I didn't mean to do this. I…" He stood and turned his back on me. "I'm a monster, Red." He grabbed his pants and pulled them on. "You deserve someone better than me. I'll send in someone to tend to your wounds."

Without another word, he turned and fled the room. Vincenzo left me on the bed, broken and confused. Despite the utter terror I felt, I didn't want anyone else to touch me.

I wanted *him*.

Easing off the bed, I hissed through the pain as I quickly gathered my things. I stuffed everything in my jacket pocket, composed myself, then hurried from the room before anyone else came in. Several patrons watched me as I beelined for the elevator, but no one tried to stop me. Once I stepped inside, I let myself crumble again.

Maybe he was right.

Maybe he was a *monster*.

eleven

VINCENZO

"We have Jorge," Massimo's voice filtered through the line.

"I'll be there in five." I hurried out of my place and hopped onto my bike.

The restaurant was closed today, thank God. I wasn't in any shape to be around people—unless it was to cause pain. I lost control with Red, tearing her flesh like she was another victim of my blade. The look in her eyes would be permanently carved into my memory. I'd put fear into her beautiful green gaze—she'd been afraid of *me*. I'd never had a sub afraid during or after role play. What I'd done to her... was unforgivable.

I parked, hurried inside Discoteca, and made my way down to the basement. Donny was standing against the wall watching Jorge, who was tied to a chair.

He smirked when he saw me, "Well, you're fucked now, Jorge." Donny pushed off the wall and moved to the opposite side.

I stepped into Jorge's view, his eyes widening with fear. "Where's Dmitri?"

"Fuck you."

"You didn't win Jorge. We found Katya, and she's safe now. I can't say the same for you."

I started toward him, but the door burst open, revealing Matias and Massimo. I watched as a myriad of emotions crossed Matias' face.

"Control your anger. We still need to know where Dmitri is." Massimo held onto Matias, halting him in place.

I sneered as I flipped the serrated blade I pulled from my boot. "Tell me, Jorge. Where is he hiding?"

Jorge spat onto the floor, causing Matias to tense. "Look who it is… the boyfriend." The muscles in Matias' neck flexed and tightened as he fought to restrain himself from lashing back. "How's that pretty little woman? Mmmm… Every time I drove my fist into her, I she cried out for you, making my cock harden with the thrill. But her cries finally stopped when she realized you weren't coming. It gives me immense pleasure knowing I ruined that bitch's cunt for any man who follows behind me."

I watched as Matias leaped from Massimo's hold. His body hit Jorge with such force, they both fell to the floor in a tangle. The wooden chair splintered beneath Jorge as he laid beneath him, gasping for air. Matias' fists connected with his face. The sound of bone on bone filled the room as he drew back and repeated his blows. Jorge didn't stand a chance against Matias's rage as he pummeled him in quick succession.

"You will never touch anyone again," Matias grunted as his knuckles connected, tearing into the tender flesh along Jorge's cheekbone. Matias wrapped his hand around his throat, cutting off the air supply. Jorge clawed at his binds, trying to get his hands free with no luck. "You didn't break her. She told me to tell you, you didn't win. You're just Dmitri's bitch—a bitch he left behind to die." Matias applied more pressure. "I want you near death, then I'll stand by and watch as the blade carves into your pathetic flesh. In your weakened state, you won't be able to fight. You'll be forced to watch as he slices into your body over and over again. You don't deserve death—it's too easy. I *want* you to suffer—no, I *need* you to suffer. I want you to feel the fear that Katya felt every time you put your hands on her."

"Matias." Massimo placed his hand on his shoulder. "That's enough. Let go."

Matias came back to himself, realizing Jorge had gone unconscious. "Shit. Did I kill him?"

"No. He passed out. Let's get him in the chair over here." Massimo pointed to another chair off to the side. I leaned against the wall, watching them as they dragged him onto the wooden perch. "Wake up." Massimo backhanded Jorge, rousing him from his unconscious state. "Tell me where Dmitri is."

Jorge mumbled. "Fuck you." His body giving out on him from the beating Matias had unleashed.

"Vincenzo." Massimo turned as he called out to me.

I was already walking toward them, eager to take out the rage I had been trying to contain. "If he doesn't answer you, kill him. I don't have time for his pathetic ass. You fucking had my brother. You tried to ruin Matias' woman. I don't have sympathy for people like you."

Jorge mumbled between the pained breaths he was taking. "You think I care about death?" He struggled for air. "There is nothing left for me now. Dmitri will kill me anyway."

I yanked him off the chair and tossed him against the table. Wedging my body against his back, I pressed his head to the surface. "Matias. Do you want this quick, or should I make it last?"

Matias looked at Jorge and grunted. "I don't care what you do to him. He doesn't deserve death, but Katya deserves a life free of fear. Do whatever you want. I'm done."

Massimo nodded his head toward me and then waved Matias toward the door. "You should go home to Katya. This mother-fucker is going to get what he deserves, I promise."

"Jorge," Matias called out before leaving the room. "Tell Dmitri hello when you meet him in Hell."

I waited until the door closed and leaned in to whisper in Jorge's ear. "You like to beat women? Well, I like to cut motherfuckers up. I hope you've made peace with death because this will not be quick. I want you to feel everything I do so you can feel what Katya did every time you hit her… every time you forced yourself on her and she begged for you to stop." I ran the blade across his cheek, drawing blood.

"You're sick." Jorge gasped beneath me as the blade trailed down his neck.

"You have no idea. Don't you know who I am?" I pressed the metal into his shoulder, the tip digging beneath the skin. "I'm La Lama."

His raspy intake of breath confirmed he realized his fate was much worse than death. I pressed deeper, the end of the knife piercing through to the table beneath him.

"I love carving up assholes like you."

"Kill me. You won't get what you want."

"I don't need you to tell me where he is. We know Dmitri is back in Vegas somewhere. It won't be long until we find him, and I will do to him what I'm going to do to you."

His screams filled the room as I worked my blade like an expert. I wanted to punish him for all the things he had done to Katya and Antonio. They deserved retribution. I wouldn't stop until I felt like I'd given him what he deserved. Every slice, every stick of the metal into his flesh, gave me a charge of power. Power I'd desperately needed and craved.

"Vincenzo," Donny's voice cut through the bloodlust that had taken over. "I think you've made your point."

I glanced down at what was left of the man and took a step back. He was completely unrecognizable and had stopped breathing some time ago. I wiped my blade across my pants and stuffed it back into my boot.

"Can you take care of this?"

"Yeah. You can go get cleaned up. Maybe you should do that before you go upstairs?" Donny looked at my arms, which were stained almost black from the dried blood.

"Probably." I walked to the sink at the back of the room and scrubbed my hands until the water ran clear. I was slowly losing it. I'd become so lost in the mutilation of Jorge that I hadn't realized when he'd finally ceased to exist. Finding the spare clothes Massimo left behind, I changed out of my ruined ones. Once I finished, I tossed them into the trash and, without another word, I walked out of the basement.

It wasn't until I pulled into my driveway that I realized I had even left the club. Darkness clouded my vision.

I'd hurt my sub because I lost control and now…

I barely recognized the man I was becoming.

twelve

RILEY

MY ENTIRE BODY HURT. Every move or twist I made sent pain lancing through my body. I avoided Vincenzo as much as I could, but his gaze seemed to follow me everywhere. I had called in sick for two days, but I couldn't keep avoiding work and finally returned.

He stood behind me, watching as I bent slowly to retrieve something.

"Are you alright?"

"Yes. Why do you ask?"

"I've been watching you and something seems off. Are you sure you're well enough to be back at work? I mean, you were sick for two days." His tone was suspicious, and I couldn't look at him out of fear he'd see the truth in my eyes.

"I think you should stop watching me and start cooking. If anyone is off today, it's you."

Turning to grab a plate, I slipped on some spilled water, but Vincenzo was quick on his feet. He wrapped an arm around my waist and jerked me against him. There was no hiding the pain from him. I screamed out as my back pressed into him, the tattered flesh I was hiding beneath my clothes igniting with a fire that raged across my skin.

"What the *fuck*?" Vincenzo carried me out of the kitchen, past the other chefs, and deposited me on my feet in his office. Slamming the door shut, he turned to face me. "You're hurt. I knew it. What happened, Riley?"

"Nothing. It's nothing. I should just go home." I started past him, but he latched onto my arm and stopped me. "I'll be fine in a day or two." I tried to jerk out of his hold, but he wasn't having it.

Pinning my arms above my head, his fingers wrapped around my wrists, holding them in place as his free hand ripped my shirt up. His quick intake of breath and the silence that followed had me breathing fast.

I closed my eyes and wiggled out of his hold.

"Don't." I jerked the material down, covering the marks.

"How did I not know? All this time, it was you." He paced the floor as he ran his hand through his hair. "I did that to you." He waved to my body. "How come you didn't tell me it was you? Why did you lie all this time?"

"I was afraid. That part of my life is separate—it always has been. After the first time we were together, I wanted to let myself have the fantasy. I didn't want to risk losing what we shared at Fantasia if you knew it was me."

He took a step toward me. "Pull up your shirt."

"No." I held my hand out. "Please. Let it go."

"Riley. Don't fucking deny me. I shouldn't have left you alone that night. I was ashamed of myself for losing control. Now, do as I say, and let me see." He clenched his jaw as he spoke.

Seeing the pain in his eyes, I nodded and closed my eyes. I unbuttoned my top and slipped it off, letting it fall to the floor. My skin was crisscrossed with angry red welts that were littered all the way down my abdomen and dipped beneath my skirt.

"Fuck." He stepped forward and reached out. I hissed as his fingers traced the swollen flesh. Vincenzo pressed his palm against my belly, and I flinched.

"Stop."

"Did you clean these?" The softness in his tone had me opening my eyes to look at him.

"Yes."

"Not good enough." He pulled his hand free and stepped back. "Put your shirt back on. We're leaving."

"What? We can't just leave in the middle of dinner service, Vincenzo."

"Yes. We can." He grabbed his keys and pulled the door open. "The other chefs are more than capable of finishing up, and if not, I will close the fucking restaurant. I need to see to those marks, and I can't do it here."

"No, I'm fine, just tender. I'll be okay."

He leaned forward, his face inches from mine. "This is why you were out sick?"

I sighed. "Yes."

Reaching down, he fisted my shirt and handed it to me. "Get your things. I won't take no for an answer."

I shook my head, knowing I would not win this argument. "Fine." I tugged the white blouse back on and followed him out into the restaurant.

He briefed the other line chefs, telling them I hurt myself when I slipped in the kitchen and that he was taking me to be looked at. After grabbing my bag, he shocked me by scooping me off my feet and carrying me outside.

"It's not ideal, but we'll take my bike. Think you can hold on, or will it hurt too much?" He pushed his helmet down on my head and climbed on.

"I think I can manage." I straddled the bike behind him and gripped his waist. "How far is your place? Should you be riding without a helmet?"

"I'll be fine. It's not far. Hold on." Vincenzo flicked his eyes over his shoulders as I wrapped my arms around his waist. Once he was certain I was secured behind him, he took off, navigating the streets of Vegas until he pulled into a one-story bungalow.

"Your house is beautiful." I tugged the helmet from my head and cradled it in my arm.

"Thank you." He kicked the bike stand down and killed the engine. "My father had it built for me."

He eased me off the back, set the helmet on the seat, and carried me inside. I couldn't believe how magnificent it was.

I honestly didn't expect such a stunning house from a bachelor.

"Take off your shirt, Riley." His voice cut through the silence, snapping my attention to him.

"Don't you think we should talk first?"

"We can talk, as I tend to your skin."

I followed him down the hall into what I assumed was his master bedroom. The gray walls were offset by a massive four-post bed covered in a black duvet.

"Vincenzo, why am I here?"

"I fucked up, Riley. I lost control and hurt you. I need to do this, or I will never forgive myself." He moved into the bathroom and gathered supplies.

"You wouldn't have even known it was me if I hadn't slipped."

"You're right, and I want to know why that is? And don't give me some bullshit that it's because you keep that part of your life separate. Lie down on the bed."

Tossing my shirt to the floor, I crawled onto his plush mattress. My entire body sunk into the soft pillow top. He climbed onto the bed beside me and squirted something into his hands. I watched as he rubbed them together before placing them on my stomach. Hissing, I jerked my body beneath his touch.

"Relax, Tesoro."

His hands smoothed the cream across my flesh, rubbing in gentle circles. He stopped at the top of my skirt, his finger tracing the line that dipped beneath the waist. Unzipping it down the side, he slipped the polyester fabric down my legs and pushed it to the floor. He made a noise with his mouth, causing me to look up at him. He was staring at the marks across my legs, his eyes heavy with regret.

"Can you ever forgive me?"

"Yes. I should have used my safe word long before I did."

"Riley. This is not your fault. I did this. I told you I was a monster."

"Vincenzo." I leaned up, cupping his cheek in my hand. "Stop saying that. You want to know the reason I didn't tell you who I was? Why I kept living the lie as Red?" He leaned into my hand and nodded. "I was falling for you, and I knew if you found out who I was... who I am, you would walk away."

"You're falling for me?"

"Yes, I am. It's wrong on so many levels, but I thought if I could keep you as Red, nothing would change."

"I don't understand, Riley. Why would I walk away from you? It's you who should run."

"You don't understand." I turned my head so he couldn't see the pain in my eyes.

"Then help me understand. What could make me walk away from you? I told you who I was. You know my family, yet you think there's something about you that would make me turn away?" He shifted off me to grab more ointment.

"Yes." I took that opportunity and slipped out from beneath him to stand. Feeling extremely vulnerable, I paced his floor.

"I'm not who you think I am, and when I tell you, everything changes, Vincenzo. *Everything*."

He sat watching me pace like a scared kitten. Everything I'd worked for came down to this moment. Telling him the truth risked losing him and destroying my entire career, but I didn't care. Standing in front of him, I knew without a doubt that I was in love with him.

"Riley, just tell me. Whatever it is, we can work through it."

"I don't know about that." I took a steadying breath and blew it out. "Just know, what I am about to tell you changes nothing. I meant what I said. I'm falling in love with you."

"Are you married? Is that it?"

"No…" I swallowed the bile in my throat. "I'm not married." I took a breath and closed my eyes. "I'm a federal agent."

He blinked, as if unsure he heard me. "What did you say?"

"I'm with the FBI, Vincenzo. I was sent in undercover to gather evidence against you and your brothers."

He stood frozen in his spot, staring at me.

"Did you hear what I said, Vincenzo? I'm an undercover agent."

thirteen

VINCENZO

I WAS DREAMING—I had to be. There was no way Riley had just confessed to being an FBI agent.

"Did you hear what I said, Vincenzo? I'm an undercover agent," she repeated.

My gaze narrowed in on her and I blinked.

"Are you serious?"

"Yes."

"I need a minute." I walked out of my room, leaving her alone so I could gather my thoughts. Grabbing my phone out of my pocket, I dialed Alec. Surely, he could tell me she was lying.

"Vin, what's up?"

"Alec. Have you found anything on Riley?"

"No. I was going to call you tomorrow and tell you. It's like she didn't exist before last year. No social media, nothing."

I scrubbed my hand down my face. "Fuck."

"What is it, Boss?"

"Nothing. I'll call you later. If you find anything, you call me. And remember, my brothers don't need to know about this."

He sighed into the phone. "Sure. Are you alright?"

"Yeah. I gotta go." I tossed my phone onto the table in the kitchen and leaned against the counter.

How had I missed this? I was a fucking Anastasi. This shit didn't slip by us, yet the woman sitting in my room had managed to infiltrate our private lives completely undetected.

"Vincenzo." Her soft voice filled the kitchen.

Turning to her, I folded my arms across my chest. She was standing in nothing but one of my shirts, which I assumed she took from my closet.

"What do you want from me, Riley?"

"Look. I know this looks bad, but you have to understand..." She bit her lip as she spoke. "Everything has changed. I was going to tell you."

"When exactly? Were you going to say something as you arrested me or after you arrested my brothers?"

"Please. Listen to me. I didn't mean for this to happen. You were just supposed to be a job. I wasn't supposed to fall in love with you."

"Are you telling me you haven't provided your department with information about my family?"

She nibbled at her lip, anxiety pouring off her in waves.

"That's exactly what I'm saying."

"I don't believe you, Riley."

"I know you don't, but I swear I've told them nothing. I couldn't."

I stepped toward her, causing her to step back out of fear. She backed into the wall and froze as I crowded her in.

"Why didn't you? You know enough information to do considerable damage not to just me, but Massimo and Antonio."

"I told you. I couldn't. I see you for more than what's in the file I have on you. Everything you do is to help others… even if it's illegal."

I shook my head. "You wouldn't say that if you knew the real me."

She reached up and brushed her palm across my cheek. "Yes, I would."

"Really? You'd still say you love me if you knew how many people I've killed? You'd love me knowing I was the man everyone called to clean up their problems?"

Tears pooled in her eyes, the sight gutting me when it shouldn't have.

"I don't care. That was your past. Please… don't push me away." Her quick intake of breath and the whisper from her lips had my cock hard as a rock.

"You don't care?" I laughed as I wedged my knee between her legs. "A woman of the law doesn't care that I've killed people for money. That I was the man people called when no one else could do the job." Her eyes dilated as she watched my lips move closer. "Being with me could end your career. Are you alright with that?"

"I don't know."

I fastened my mouth over hers in a searing kiss. Her hands fisted my hair as I fucked her lips with mine. Gripping her ass in my palms, I lifted her and pressed her back into the wall. She winced slightly, but her legs wrapped around me. Her warm center pressed against my stomach. Even through her panties, I could feel her heat.

"We can't do this, Vincenzo." Her words were telling me no, but the moans against my mouth told me otherwise.

I should have sent her on her way, but I couldn't. I wanted to teach her a lesson—but more so than that, I wanted to own her fucking soul. Lifting her from the wall, I walked her back to my room and threw her down on my bed. I stripped off my clothes, then ripped off the shirt she was wearing and tossed it aside.

My tongue traced the reddened skin, eliciting a huff out of her. Pinning her legs to the mattress, I snatched the dainty lace material from her core and buried myself between her legs. My tongue licked the seam of her pussy, dipping in and out of her folds. Her body thrashed beneath me as she tried to pull free of my assault on her wet hole.

"Don't move," I growled against her cleft, biting down hard on her clit as she screamed out her release. I slurped every last drop of her cum before crawling up her body and pinning her arms above her head.

"I take what I want, Red. Does your file tell you that?" I leaned down and captured one of her lace-clad nipples in my mouth. Even through the scant fabric, I could taste the sweetness of her flesh. Just as I bit down on the pert tip, I speared my cock inside her. She cried out from the forceful intrusion, stilling beneath me before finally adjusting to my girth.

"You can pretend to be the villain, Vincenzo, but I know it's not who you are." Her body contorted beneath me as she thrust my cock deeper inside her.

We began moving as one, our bodies in step with what we desperately needed from one another—me needing to dominate her and her needing to prove she could handle all of me. I pumped into her, claiming her mouth with ferocity. Her entire body seized as her inner walls tightened around my shaft. As she fell over into the abyss, my cock jerked and exploded deep inside her womb. Panting, I collapsed beside her and tugged her into my arms.

"You're *mine* now, Riley… federal agent or not. We're going to have to figure this out. If we don't, you know where it will lead."

She nodded against my chest. "Can you just hold me for now?"

"Go to sleep, Tesoro. We can talk more tomorrow."

Her body relaxed against me as her breaths evened out. I knew this would likely end badly—how could it not?

The road only had one path that set us both free… and I wasn't sure she would take it.

My body was wrapped in a blanket of warmth when I woke. Vincenzo was sleeping soundly with his arm holding me snug against him. I slowly wiggled myself out from under his grasp and sat up on the edge of the bed. My head spun with confusion as I stared at the sleeping man beside me. Standing, I grabbed his discarded T-shirt and made my way into the kitchen.

My entire existence hinged on me bringing this family down. For years, we'd worked on building a case against the Anastasi's for gun running and money laundering. We had suspicions they had ties to La Lama—a man wanted for the death of hundreds. The people he killed were men who deserved their fates, just not at the hands of a vigilante.

Spotting my chef's coat on the floor, I bent to pick it up. I tugged my phone out and sighed. It was dead. Scanning the counter in the kitchen, I spotted his charger. As soon as I plugged in my phone, it beeped with a dozen messages. Each one read the same—Agent Jackson had been trying to contact me. I leaned into the counter and pressed his contact.

Agent Jackson's pissed-off voice barked into the phone. "Agent Lawson, where in the hell have you been?"

"Sorry. My phone died, and I fell asleep."

"I was worried we were going to have to send someone to your place."

"No, that's unnecessary. What's the matter? Why so many calls?"

"We got word that Dmitri Ivanov is in town. Have you been able to determine a link between him and the Anastasis?"

"No…" I jumped at the sound of a throat clearing behind me. My eyes connected with Vincenzo. He was leaning against the doorway, wearing only a pair of fitted black boxers. "I'm not sure there is anything to connect."

"Bullshit. There has to be something."

Vincenzo watched me closely, listening to every word I said. I wasn't lying—technically. I hadn't found anything that would help put his family in jail. Granted, I knew his family was searching for Ivanov. That detail wasn't important.

"Look, I told you there isn't anything. I won't make something up to put an innocent man in jail."

"If you don't find something, and soon, Pritz is going to pull you and go another route."

"I'll find something. Give me time."

"You better."

I laid the phone down on the counter and sighed. Things were unraveling faster than I expected.

"You lied to him."

I turned toward Vincenzo and smiled. "Not really. I have nothing that ties you to Ivanov in the way he wants."

"Why did you lie, though?"

I fidgeted with my hands as he stepped forward and braced me against the counter.

"Why are you risking your career for me?"

"You know why."

"Say it, Riley. I need to hear it from you."

I cupped his cheek and ran my thumb over his lips.

"I've fallen in love with you. It shouldn't have happened. When I met you at the club, I thought… no, I hoped I could live the fantasy with you there, since an actual life with you wasn't possible." I laced my hands in his hair and pressed a kiss to his lips. "I was supposed to dismantle you and your family. My entire purpose was to prove you were La Lama, but that seems stupid now."

Vincenzo's body seized at the mention of La Lama. His eyes had gone vacant, as though he was trapped in a memory.

"Did I say something wrong? I mean, you're not La Lama, so this shouldn't matter."

"I'm not who you think I am, Riley. Before you give yourself to me, you need to understand you'd be giving yourself to the Devil."

"Would you stop saying that?"

He pushed up from the table, knocking a chair to the floor. The sound reverberated through the kitchen, causing me to jump.

"Vincenzo…" I jumped up and ran after him.

"VINCENZO…" HER FOOTSTEPS BEAT AGAINST THE FLOOR AS she chased me down the hall. "Wait. *Please.*"

"You should arrest me now." I shoved my fingers through my hair.

"Jesus Christ, can you just stop for a minute?"

I turned, causing her to bump into me. My arms instinctively wrapped around her to prevent her from falling on her ass.

"Why are you running from me?"

"I am the monster you think I am. Can you accept that you're in love with a murderer?"

"Who you were years ago doesn't matter to me. What matters is who you are right now."

"I've killed men, Riley." I narrowed my eyes, my eyebrow arching with my words. "As recently as last week."

"Oh." Her eyes cast down, her forehead creasing with confusion.

I slipped my finger beneath her chin, lifting her eyes to meet mine.

"Dmitri came after my family. He killed Miguel Angel's sister and tried to pin it on me. And if that wasn't enough, he tried to kidnap my sister, then succeeded in taking Antonio. The men I've murdered were his lackeys, but the law doesn't care. Being with me would mean turning your back on everything you stand for."

"Look, I know this,"—she jerked her finger between us—"doesn't make any sense, but I can't stop how I feel."

"Do you understand what it will mean to be with me? I won't change who I am, and my family will always be my family."

"I won't ask you to change."

"Riley." I curved my hand behind her head and tilted it back. "There will come a day when you'll have to decide. I don't think you understand that."

"Can we just worry about what's happening now? If today is all you can give me, then talking about tomorrow is pointless."

Her lips crashed into mine as she pushed me into the bedroom. My hands went to her ass, yanking her off her feet and taking control. I walked us to the bed and laid her down, this time intending to take my time. My body covered hers as our mouths fought for dominance. I broke the kiss and pushed off the bed.

"Hold still." I walked to my closet and retrieved several ties. "Strip off your shirt, Riley."

I watched in awe as she stood and pulled the shirt off, tossing it to the floor. She was bare beneath the top, smiling as she climbed back onto the bed. Her skin was flushed a beautiful shade of pink, the red stripes prominently on display. I ran my fingers down the lash marks, making her skin pebble beneath my touch. Tying the silken fabric around her wrists, I fastened them to the corner posts. I repeated the same action with her feet, spreading her legs wide. Her pretty pink pussy glistened with her desire, begging to be touched.

"Please." Her plea drifted through the room, sending a bolt of need to my cock.

"I'm going to show you what being mine is like." I pressed my hands to her thighs, massaging the marked flesh. My fingers danced down her legs, pushing them farther apart and shoving my fingers into her core.

"This pussy belongs to me." She whimpered, pulling against the restraints. "Say it, Riley. Say this pussy is mine."

"It's yours. My pussy is yours."

I dove in, licking and sucking her tender folds into my mouth. Her flavor assaulted my senses as my tongue lapped at her center. I could feel her body quivering at every touch. When I finally slipped in a finger, her walls contracted around my digit as if not to let go.

"Let go, Tesoro."

I drove my fingers in and out, sucking on her clit. Her tiny bundle of nerves set off a chain of quakes, signaling the release she was chasing. Using my teeth, I applied a small amount of pressure to her bud, driving her over the edge. She screamed out, her orgasm washing over her. I eagerly lapped her juices, biting her flesh as she cried out in bliss. Nipping at her thigh, I climbed her body, placing kisses on the marks I'd left previously.

"I cannot tell you how sorry I am for doing this to you, Riley."

"Stop. Don't do that after giving me a mind-blowing orgasm, Vincenzo. I know you didn't mean it. Now…" she tilted her head up and held my gaze. "Are you going to fuck me or not?"

I pressed my hands to her chest, pinching her pert nipple. My hand cupped her pussy, my fingers dipping back between her folds.

"I plan to worship your body as long as I have you, Tesoro."

Pulling my fingers out, I licked them as she watched. My fingers wrapped around her neck as I lined my cock up with her center.

"Hold on, baby girl. It's about to get rough."

I thrust inside her as my hand tightened around her throat. Her eyes closed in ecstasy as I pounded into her. Her binds tightened as her body rocked beneath me. I wouldn't last long. My need to claim her was too powerful.

"Can you come for me?"

"Yes," she whimpered, her pussy fluttering around my shaft.

Slipping my free hand between us, I pressed my thumb to the swollen pearl, causing her walls to choke down around my shaft. The sensation of being squeezed made my balls tightened and the orgasm to burst free.

"Fuck!" I roared into the room as my cock erupted inside her. Pounding into her, my seed spurted into her womb like a fire hose dousing a flame. I collapsed with my cock still buried inside her, then untied her arms, allowing her to wrap them around my neck.

"Vincenzo." She whispered against my cheek, her breaths coming out in pants. "You're crushing me."

Shifting my weight, my dick slipped out of her as I rolled onto my back. She sat up and untied her legs, tossing the neck ties to the floor, then rolled against me and rested her head in the crook of my shoulder.

She pressed a kiss to my flesh. "What happens now?"

"We take a nap, then shower. The restaurant has to be opened today."

Her heavy sigh tickled my skin. "You know what I mean, Vincenzo."

"How about we take it day by day?"

"Okay. Can you promise me something?"

I closed my eyes, afraid of what she was going to ask. "I don't know, Tesoro."

"If you find Dmitri, let me take him in. I can't protect you if you kill him."

"You know who I am, Riley. That's a promise I can't make you. For now, we'll take it one day at a time, but you know as well as I do, there will come a point when we have to decide."

"Yeah, I do."

I held her tighter, not wanting to let her go... even though I knew deep down that's where this would lead.

fifteen

RILEY

"PRITZ IS PISSED you have nothing. He wants you to bug the restaurant."

"What the fuck, Jackson?" There was no way I was going to do that. I'd be ousting myself right along with the Anastasis. "You can't be serious."

"Are you getting too close to your boss, Riley?" Jackson's eyes narrowed. "It feels like you're evading your purpose."

"No, of course not." My palms were sweating as I closed my fingers into a fist beneath the table.

"Good." Jackson slid the tiny listening device across the table to me and smiled. "Just put it in the office when you can and press this button. Maybe we'll pick up something you're not privy to."

"Fine." My gut coiled with disgust. I'd spent years trying to get where I was with the FBI, but I was about to betray everything my badge stood for. "I'll do it as soon as I can. Anything else?"

"Yeah. It's been confirmed. Dmitri Ivanov is back in Vegas. Carmichael's team spotted him outside of the city. I don't know what's going on, but I have a feeling it's big and I have a feeling your boss is at the center of it all."

"What if we're wrong?"

Jackson laughed, but realized my expression was serious.

"Wait. You're serious? Come on, Lawson, you know the Anastasis are the biggest mob family in Vegas. Ivanov would be the perfect crime partner. With his contacts in Russia, the Anastasi's would be untouchable if they aligned with him."

"What if they are at war with him? I mean…" I shifted in the booth. "What if the Anastasis are actually at odds with Ivanov? Maybe we're going at this all wrong. They could be the key to bringing down one of the biggest criminals the FBI has seen in a while."

"Do you hear yourself? Riley, just plant the bug. Work the angle you're supposed to. I'm not throwing years of investigation down the drain because you have a whim."

"Fine." I ran my hands through my hair. "You're right." I glanced at my watch and sighed. "I have to get to work if you don't want the boss wondering what I've been doing."

"Okay. Remember,"—he tapped his ear— "we'll be listening. If there is a connection between them, we'll find it."

I left the café, disgusted with myself. The longer I spent with Vincenzo, the more I wanted nothing to do with this case. I was seeing him and his family in a different light. Sure, what they did was outside the law, but they were keeping scum off the streets—something law enforcement couldn't do.

Parking my car near my apartment, I walked to the restaurant. I wasn't about to plant the bug without telling Vincenzo first. I had to do it, but I would do what I could to protect him. I shoved it into my pocket and pulled open the restaurant door. The air felt charged as I stalked across the dining room toward the back office. I couldn't explain why, but I felt as if I was betraying someone—I just wasn't sure who that was anymore.

Vincenzo was seated in the private room with his brothers. I tried to sneak past before anyone noticed I was there, but three pairs of eyes locked onto mine, freezing me in place.

"Agent Lawson." Massimo Anastasi cocked an eyebrow at me, his tone laced with venom. Breaking his stare, my eyes sought Vincenzo, who was already moving toward me.

"I…" I stepped back from the open doorway.

"Riley."

Vincenzo's deep tone caused me to stumble. Strong arms wrapped around me, keeping me from tumbling backward on my ass.

"Agent Lawson." This time, it was Antonio Anastasi who spoke. "Please come in and have a seat." He motioned to an empty chair at the end of the table.

Vincenzo clung to my hand as he led me toward the table. I glanced around at the two men, watching me with suspicion as I sat down.

"Give me one reason I shouldn't end your very existence right now," Massimo bellowed.

"Fratello," Vincenzo growled, pressing his hands into my shoulders to hold me in place. He sensed my need to bolt. "We discussed this."

"We did, but I need to hear it from her. I need to know if she's a threat."

"Well?" Antonio kicked his feet on top of the table and crossed his arms across his chest. His demeanor was completely opposite of Massimo's. He looked… amused.

I leaned backward, looking up into Vincenzo's face.

"You told them?"

"I did, Tesoro. They needed to know what was going on."

I pressed my hands to my face to calm my nerves. Here I sat, in front of the three most powerful men in Las Vegas, and I was holding a fucking bug in my pocket.

"Well." I slipped my hand into my pocket and pulled it out, tossing it to the table. "Let's start with the fact I was ordered to bug this place." Massimo slammed his fist on the table, making the listening device bounce against the wooden surface. "Look, I'm not sure where to start." I scanned their faces and swallowed. "I've been working with the FBI for the last three years."

"Fuck," Antonio grunted. "Are you even a chef?"

"Yes. Or at least I was a long time ago. Right out of high school, I went to culinary school. I wanted to be like my dad —a chef." I swallowed the bile rising in my throat as I recounted the memories I'd spent the last six years trying to bury. "I worked alongside him at his restaurant. It was surreal being just twenty and commanding a team of chefs, but I did."

"How does a woman go from being a chef to an agent with the FBI?"

"It's simple. My father, Robert Murphy, was murdered. Shot in cold blood. The police determined he was in the wrong place at the wrong time. He'd been caught in the middle of a hit gone wrong. That night, Rebecca Murphy died as well. I walked out of the hospital and applied to the police academy. I became Riley Lawson and never looked back. I was top of my class and was quickly recruited to the undercover division. I worked my ass off, determined to find my father's killer. It wasn't until I was approached by an agent with the FBI, I considered becoming an agent. Apparently, my investigation had piqued their interest enough to bring me on as part of a joint task force to locate who I now know as La Lama. It's believed he is the reason my dad is dead."

Antonio's eyes widened as he looked at Vincenzo. "Fratello?"

"What?" I glanced between the two brothers, who seemed to be sharing some kind of silent turmoil. "What am I missing?"

Vincenzo turned from the table, putting his back to me. He stood with his hands braced against the wall with his head down.

"La Lama doesn't kill using a gun."

"How could you know that?" I glanced back at Massimo, who was watching me with what looked like sympathy.

"Do you love our brother?" Antonio spoke, making my gaze snap to his.

"What does that have to do with La Lama?" I watched as the two men stood.

"*Everything*," Massimo whispered, his eyes closing. "We will figure out what to do with that." He pointed to the bug. "But first…" He pressed his hand to Vincenzo's shoulder. "We will give you two a moment."

I watched as they left the room, leaving me alone with Vincenzo.

"Vincenzo. How do you know how La Lama kills his victims?"

"You're an agent, Riley. You should know La Lama prefers his blade."

"I know that, but reports say he pulled a gun when the man he was there to kill turned the tables."

"They're wrong."

"I don't understand." I ran my hand through my hair, my heart beating against my chest like a pack of wild horses running across the fields.

"You do, Riley. I told you I was a monster."

sixteen

VINCENZO

"LA LAMA WOULD NEVER taint his reputation using a gun. It's too impersonal." I watched as the realization dawned on her face.

"What are you saying?" Riley stood and paced the floor.

"Can you tell me where your father was killed?"

"Outside his restaurant. I had the night off when it happened. The police report said he was the victim of a robbery, yet nothing was taken. He was one of two victims. The other dead body was the supposed robber. They said my father had stabbed him with a butcher knife just before the bullet took his life."

"Michael Bodachi was no robber."

The night flooded back into my conscious, taking me back to the moment I walked away from being La Lama.

"La Lama." Michael sneered as he walked around me.

"Bodachi." I spun the blade between my fingers, taunting him. "You knew this was coming. No one betrays the family and lives."

"I see they've sent their prodigal son to end my life. I knew you'd come for me." Michael pulled out his pistol and aimed it at my chest. "But I plan on taking you to Hell with me."

"You think I fear death?" Laughing, I stepped closer, ready to meet my maker. "I crave the freedom it would give me."

A noise to my right caused us both to glance at the interruption. We were secluded in an alleyway off the main road. A man stepped into the dim light, wielding a large cutting knife.

"Who the fuck is out here?" he demanded, unaware of the danger he was stepping into.

The shot echoed off the brick walls, causing me to lunge toward Bodachi. The stranger fell to the ground, his knife tumbling from his grip onto the pavement.

My blade sliced through Bodachi's gut, severing his spine as it protruded through his back. His body crumpled to the ground, my blade slipping out of his flesh as he did. I turned toward the innocent man, praying I could do something.

"Hey." I kneeled beside him, cradling his head in my hands. "Stay with me." I slipped my phone out and dialed 911, praying they would arrive fast enough. He didn't deserve his death—especially not in a dirty alleyway.

"Please…" he gurgled in his own blood, trying to speak. "My daughter."

I looked around, wondering if she was going to burst out of the door and find us here.

"Is she inside?"

"No..."

"Hey, stop talking. Save your energy." The sirens sounded off in the distance, reminding me I couldn't stay. "Look, I can't be here when they get here."

He reached up and gripped my hand. "You can still find the light."

"Vincenzo?"

Riley pulled me from the memory.

"Riley, I'm La Lama. I didn't kill your dad, but I might as well have. I left him to die in that alley so the police wouldn't find me."

"You're La Lama."

Her pained whisper punched me in the gut.

"When I told you that you'd be giving yourself to the Devil, I meant it."

She stood beside me, waiting for me to say something more, but what more was there? I was the reason her father was dead. I was the reason she'd become the person she was.

"You didn't kill my father."

I looked into her eyes, eyes that held deep sorrow and pain—an emotion I was responsible for putting there.

"I didn't save him either." She reached out to touch me, but I jerked away. "Did you hear me, Riley? I'm the reason your father is dead. I watched him bleed out on the pavement that night. I stayed with him as long as I could, but finally left to save myself."

"Michael Bodachi is the man who shot my father. Not you. And there was nothing you could have done for my dad. The bullet nicked his heart. He was dead by the time they got him to the hospital."

"You know, he called out for you."

"He did?" Her eyes let the tears splash down her cheeks.

"Yes. He called out for you. I thought maybe you were inside, but you weren't. He told me I could still find the light. I didn't know what that meant, but I spent the last few years trying to find out. He's the reason I let La Lama die that night. I no longer wanted that man I was."

She stepped forward, pinning me with a hopeful glare. "And did you find the light?"

I held her gaze, the green of her eyes drawing me in. They were lined with the most beautiful blue ring, like a starry night, making it easy to get lost in them.

"I thought maybe I had,"—he sighed— "but now I'm afraid I've lost it again."

"Vincenzo… don't you see? This changes everything for me." She fisted her hands at her sides. "I joined the task force so I could bring my father's killer to justice. But I was wrong. He was already dead."

"This does change everything… just not in the way you want it to."

"No, it doesn't." She grabbed my hand. "Love doesn't just stop, and I fell in love with you. Your past be damned."

"You shouldn't love me, Riley. Everything I touch becomes dark. I won't be the reason your light is extinguished."

"Don't I get a say in this? It's my life, goddamn it." I jerked my hand from hers. "Why are you so afraid to let someone in?"

"I don't deserve love, Riley."

"Everyone deserves love. When I look at you, I don't see a monster. I see a man who hides so much pain, he can't see the light buried deep inside." She straightened her spine, her head held high. "Well, I see it. Let me in, Vincenzo. Let me show you how worthy you are of love."

What could I say to her? I didn't want to be in love with a woman who held the key to my demise, but I was. Even after hearing I was the last man to see her father alive, she demanded I let her love me. "I don't deserve this. I don't deserve you."

"Maybe not, but you have me, anyway. Can you just let go… and let me in? I shouldn't love you. I should slap cuffs on your wrists and take you in. I *can't*. I *won't*."

"Where do we go from here?"

Riley's shoulders fell. "I don't know."

"Fratello," Massimo's voice cut through the silence in the room. "Sorry to interrupt, but we need to figure out how to handle the other issue."

Riley glanced toward the table at the tiny threat.

"He's right." She walked toward the menacing bug and picked it up. "If I don't plant this, they're going to pull me off the case and find another way to bring your family down."

"We need to figure out a way to prevent that." Massimo shoved his hands into his pockets, his stance more relaxed than before. "Do you really love him?" He quirked a brow.

"Yes, I do." Riley ducked her face, her cheeks reddening with embarrassment.

"What if you put it in the kitchen? We never talk business in there."

"They're expecting me to plant it in his office."

"Fuck," Antonio grunted. "Fine. Vin, just don't have any business discussions in there."

"Riley." Massimo ran his fingers through his dark hair. "Can you try to steer them off our case?"

"I tried. I hinted that the Prizrak was causing trouble for you guys. My boss doesn't think you're working against him—he thinks you're working with him."

"What the fuck?" Antonio gritted his teeth. "That mother fucker kidnapped me. We want him dead."

"Well… they want him more than your family. Think you can deliver him to the FBI?"

"They want him even more than La Lama?"

"Ah…" She shifted nervously. "No. But I have a plan to take care of that. Look…" She held my brother's gaze. "I know you have no reason to trust me, but I promise I'm going to do everything I can to end this without you or your brothers behind bars."

"I hope you're right because no matter how my brother feels about you, I will kill you to save the Anastasi name."

Massimo's words were like a punch to my gut, but I knew he would do everything to protect his family.

"Y OU BETTER HAVE SOMETHING FOR ME?" the imposing voice of my partner barked on the other end of the phone.

"I can confirm they are not working with the Prizrak."

Jackson grew silent for a moment. "You're sure about this?"

"Yes. Dmitri Ivanov apparently kidnapped Antonio Anastasi because they refused to run something illegal for him. Since taking over, Massimo Anastasi has cut ties with anything illegal. It appears he is trying to clean up the family business."

"Fuck. Are you saying they're clean?" Jackson didn't sound convinced.

"So far, yes."

"This makes no sense. You have found nothing to link Vincenzo Anastasi to La Lama?"

I closed my eyes and recounted the way my body sang beneath his fingers the night before as our bodies tangled beneath the sheets when he made love to me.

"No… in fact." I took a breath. "I've found evidence that links La Lama to the Prizrak."

"Are you saying the Prizrak and La Lama are connected?"

"That's exactly what I'm saying."

"Bullshit. There's no way. We've got plenty of proof showing they've been in different places when La Lama strikes."

I said my next words carefully. If they were going to believe my lie, I had to make it sound good. "I found something that shows Dmitri controls the man we know as La Lama, and that isn't Vincenzo Anastasi."

"Jesus Christ. This means this investigation could be dead in the water."

"Not necessarily. I think I can convince the Anastasis into helping us bring in the Prizrak, ending Dmitri Ivanov's reign for good."

"You think the Anastasis will work with the FBI? Are you delusional? They're the most powerful crime family in Vegas. Why in the hell would they work on the right side of the law?" His mocking laugh grated on my nerves.

"Just trust me. Let me feel them out. Maybe I could get them to lead us to him without even realizing they are."

"Maybe. The bug hasn't given us anything to implicate them in the last month. Fine. I'll get Pritz to give you two weeks to work this angle. Otherwise, we're both out of jobs."

Disconnecting the call, I stared out across Vincenzo's back-yard. I'd been spending most of my time with him here. The sneaking around was hard, but being away from him was torture.

Vincenzo wrapped his arms around my waist. "Did he buy it?"

"I think so." I leaned into him and sighed.

Vincenzo's phone rang, causing him to pull away.

"What?" he barked at the caller. "When? We're on our way." He shoved it into his pocket and turned to me. His alarmed expression had my hackles raising. "We need to go to the club."

"Has something happened?" I watched for some kind of insight into his sudden mood change.

"A package has been delivered for you."

"For me?" I furrowed my brows in confusion. "I don't understand."

Vincenzo said nothing as he led me to the bedroom. His silence concerned me as we pulled on clothes and got into the car.

"Vin." I watched his face. His hardened expression freaked me out. "What aren't you telling me?"

"You need to prepare yourself. Antonio believes it's a message from Dmitri. If it is, he knows who you are and that could be dangerous for everyone involved. Did your partner hint at anything that would make you think he knows how deep you're involved?"

"No. And if Jackson suspected I was a double agent, he'd turn on me fast. He hated the fact I was given this detail."

"Look." Vincenzo parked the car in the alley behind Discoteca and laced his fingers with mine. "If this is from

Dmitri, it's going to be bad. He is known for his brutality and sending you a message will be a statement."

"I'll be fine. I knew getting involved with your family in any way would paint a target on my back. It'll be okay."

His pained look had me rethinking that I was ready for anything. I knew he wasn't telling me something about the contents waiting for us—something big. He helped me from the car and walked behind me as we stepped inside. His palm radiated heat as he pressed it to the small of my back and led me through the dim hallway. I watched in fascination as he pressed his palm to a reader and let us through the heavy door. We crept down a flight of stairs that opened to a massive room. His brothers were standing around a table.

Donny, Massimo's right-hand man, had an imposing look about him. His arms were folded across his chest, but that wasn't what had my anxiety rising. The box was opened, and Donny shook his head, halting Vincenzo in his place. It nearly knocked me down as he jerked my hand, stopping me in place as well.

"What the fuck is going on?" I glanced at each man. "What's in the box, Donny?"

"Vin." Massimo stepped toward us. "I don't think she should look."

"Riley." Vincenzo wrapped his arms around my waist and pressed a kiss to my ear. "Perhaps you should step outside."

"No." I jerked against him and pulled free. "It was addressed to me."

I stomped over to the table where the box rested. It wasn't an enormous box, but something about it screamed danger.

Every man in the room kept their eyes on me as I pressed my hands to the cardboard sides. Everything inside was telling me to walk away and let them handle whatever monster lay beneath the surface, but I couldn't.

My fingers shook as I slipped them beneath the flaps and lifted. My vision clouded and my gut churned. Bile rose, needing to be let out. Turning my head, I vomited. Dropping to the floor, my scream echoed off the walls of the room. Nothing in my training or in life could have prepared me for what was waiting inside the cardboard Hell.

I could vaguely hear voices around me as I was lifted from the floor.

"I've got you."

"Jesus Christ, Donny. Get that out of here."

Massimo was the one speaking—at least, that's what I thought. My head was trapped inside a perpetual loop of what I'd found waiting for me, something I feared I'd never get out of my mind.

"Riley." Vincenzo cupped my cheek. "Baby, can you hear me?"

"I think she's in shock." Antonio squatted beside him. "Should I call Catarina?"

"No." Vincenzo brushed his thumb across my lip. "I'll take her home. I shouldn't have let her open that fucking package. We knew it was from him. Ivanov is known for his brutality, but I never thought... *fuck.*"

"I'll make some calls." I blinked as my eyes glazed over and a door slammed shut.

"I'm so fucking sorry, Riley. I swear to you… I will stop at nothing to find him and make him pay."

"No." My voice cracked. "Not pay. Dead." I blinked, finding Vincenzo's eyes on me. "I want him dead."

"Anything for you, Tesoro… anything."

Dmitri had just made this *personal*.

eighteen

VINCENZO

I KNEW from what Antonio had told me on the phone, whatever was inside the box wasn't good. My brothers and I have seen a lot of shit in our young lives, so seeing them, along with Donny, looking like they did, I knew it was bad. Riley was strong-willed. I knew she wouldn't listen to Donny when he tried to coax her out of looking. When she opened the lid, a piece of me broke. The gut-wrenching cry she let out pierced my heart like a speeding bullet seeking a victim. I barely caught her when she collapsed to the floor.

"Massimo." I looked at my brother as I scooped her into my arms.

"We suspect he knows she's working with us to frame him. I don't understand how he found out who she really was or that —" His voice caught in his throat.

Even though Massimo was suspicious of her, family meant everything to us. Dmitri had attacked her in the most personal way. He had taken away her past in a bold and calculated method. A calling card that would leave scars for life. Even if we brought him down, this might be enough to send her away from me for good.

"Jesus Christ, Donny. Get that out of here."

"Riley." Vincenzo I cupped her cheek. "Baby, can you hear me?"

"I think she's in shock." Antonio squatted beside me. "Should I call Catarina?"

"No." I brushed my thumb across her lip. "I'll take her home. I shouldn't have let her open that fucking package. We knew it was from him. Ivanov is known for his brutality, Antonio. But I never thought... *fuck.*"

"I'll make some calls." She blinked and her eyes glazed over as the door slammed shut.

"I'm so fucking sorry, Riley. I swear to you—I will stop at nothing to find him and make him pay."

"No." Her voice cracked. "Not pay. Dead." She blinked again, finding my eyes on her. "I want him dead."

"Anything for you, Tesoro... anything," I whispered in her ear, pressing my lips to her flesh. Her body shuddered, the sobs ricocheting through my core. The sound was mournful and tragic, like a soul fracturing into a thousand tiny pieces. I wanted to break the man responsible for the pain she was feeling. If... no... not if, *when* I got my hands on him, it would feel like a thousand deaths were bestowed on him. I brushed the hair from her face. The strands had stuck to her flushed skin. Her eyes held an emptiness that I couldn't explain—an emptiness I desperately wanted to take away. "I'm so sorry. I promise you he will pay."

"Why?" Her voice broke. "She wasn't part of this."

"It's his way. Dmitri hits where it hurts. "

"How did he find her? I haven't talked—" She sucked in a breath, cutting off her words as the tears fell again.

"He has a way of finding out things, Riley. It's why he has avoided us for so long."

"Someone must have told him. The only people who know about my past are you and the FBI. This doesn't make sense." Riley stood. "Someone is working for Dmitri, and I will find out who." She started toward the door, but I reached out and grabbed her arm.

"Slow down. Massimo and the others are taking care of this. You need to take a breath."

"No," she gritted out between clenched teeth. "You need to let me go. Please." Her voice fell and her body shook.

I spun her around and pressed her against my chest. My fingers wound through her hair as I tilted her head back.

"You will listen to me, Tesoro. Do you understand?" I knew I was taking a risk exerting my dominant side on her, but if I could get her into the submissive role, she wouldn't do something dumb. "You will do as I please. Say you understand."

The beautiful green of her eyes cleared as her pupils dilated. I watched in fascination as my command washed over her, sending her into a place of confusing bliss.

"I…" Her voice trailed to a whisper.

"You what?"

"Yes, Sir." She blinked, allowing my voice to wash over her.

"I know you want vengeance, as do I, but you will not do something that will put you in further harm's way. Let my brothers deal with this for now. I am taking you back home."

Her body became languid, allowing me to pick her up and control her. I hated to be a dick, but I could see the fire in her eyes. She was allowing the anger and adrenaline to drive her right now. I couldn't let her walk out and do something stupid. Donny helped me get her in the car and buckle her up.

"We have several men on it, Vin. He won't get away with this."

I cocked my head at him. "Does she have any other family we need to notify?"

"No. It looks like Riley was it for her, even though they haven't spoken in several years."

"Fine. Please let me know when arrangements have been made."

"I'll take care of it. Massimo said Madison will meet you there. He thinks another woman may help her."

"Yes. Tell him I'll call him later." I slipped into the driver's seat and looked her over.

She was staring out into the sky, looking as lost as I felt. I was worried about her, but knew I had to handle this delicately. If her partners got wind of this incident, the FBI would beat down our front door, and we didn't need that—not when we were so close to ending this mess.

"We will be home soon." I pulled her hand into mine, not knowing how else to help her.

I wanted to erase all of her pain because I knew the chance of her falling into the darkness was high. Getting out was nearly impossible. I'd been there myself, and I was still searching for the light.

Madison was waiting in the driveway when we pulled in. She gave me a sympathetic smile as she opened Riley's door. "Come on. Let's get you inside."

"Let me help." I pushed Madison aside and scooped Riley into my arms. I carried her inside and sat her down on the couch. She'd reverted back to not talking. "I don't know how to help her." I glanced back at Madison, who was watching me.

"You can't." She stepped forward and pressed her hand against my shoulder. "When you watch someone you love ripped from your life so violently, time is the only thing that numbs the pain." My eyes found hers glistening with tears. "When I watched my mother brutally murdered in front of me, I thought I'd never heal."

I glanced at her. "But you did… heal, right?"

"Yes… because of Massimo. His love kept me from closing myself off completely and risk opening my heart gain. All you can do is love her Vin. And you do, don't you?"

I brushed Riley's loose hair from her face and cupped her cheek. "With everything I am."

"Then just love her. And in time… she'll heal, too."

nineteen

VINCENZO

I HURLED my empty drink against the wall, the glass shattering into a thousand tiny shards.

"Where is this motherfucker hiding?"

"Calm down, Vin. We know he's here in Vegas. Donny has a team of guys on it, not to mention Miguel's men are helping. We'll flush him out, I promise." Massimo tried to calm my nerves, but rage coursed through my veins, like burning hot embers.

We had convinced everyone Riley's mother had died in a tragic car accident. It seemed, for now, the FBI believed us. It was difficult for me to stay away from her, but she insisted it would blow her cover, a persona I already knew was fake. Riley had returned to her apartment the day after her mother's funeral, saying she needed some time and space, but it had been four weeks since I last saw her. I'd become a raging bull in a China shop, and everyone avoided me.

"We have to go." Antonio smiled and shoved his phone into his pocket. "That was Donny. They have one of Dmitri's men at the club."

"Let's go see what we can get out of this asshole." I couldn't wait to get my hands on this motherfucker.

I was tired of searching for Dmitri and wanted to end this once and for all. If we found Dmitri, then maybe the Feds would lay off my brothers and me. Then perhaps Riley and I could have a real chance—if that were possible. At the rate we were going, I would end up in prison, or she would end up arrested for hindering an investigation. Either way, our road was coming to some sort of end. I only hoped it could be the ending we wanted.

Massimo pulled into the alley and parked. We hurried down to the basement where Donny was waiting.

"Whatcha got, Donny?" Antonio sauntered over toward a man tied to a chair.

"This is Igor, one of Dmitri's guys."

I cocked an eyebrow at Donny and smirked. "Has he told you anything yet?"

"Nah, not a word."

"That's a shame." I slipped out the blade I kept inside my boot and turned it over in my hand. "I was really hoping I wouldn't get my hands dirty tonight."

"Fuck you." The man's thick Russian accent made him sound even more venomous than he was.

I gripped his chin, forcing his head back.

"Allow me to introduce myself. I'm Vincenzo Anastasi, but tonight, you can call me La Lama." He sucked in a breath and mumbled something unintelligible. "I see the realization dawning in your eyes. You're afraid. You know what lies ahead for you, and it *terrifies* you. You should be afraid. I'll do anything and everything to find the Prizrak... even slicing you into tiny pieces. The question is... are you willing to die for him?"

"Kill me and you will still know nothing of the Prizrak. Dying for him would be an honor." He grunted as my finger dug into his flesh.

"You heard him, Fratello. He doesn't fear death. Maybe you should change that."

"Are you sure you choose death?" I pressed the blade into his neck, digging the metal tip into the tender skin below his jaw. "Tell me where Dmitri is, and I'll spare your life."

"Go to Hell."

His words sealed his fate. I let the blistering anger take over and move my hands like they were a sculptor carving a masterpiece of hate. The blade was an extension of my soul, paving a path of vengeance through his flesh. His screams of pain were like a music to my ears. A cadence that beat to my pulse as my knife sculpted vengeance into Dmitri's man.

"Vincenzo." Massimo's voice cut through the reddened haze I was under. "That's enough."

When my eyes drifted to Igor's body, or what was left, I cringed. There was nothing left of the man—well, nothing recognizable. I'd carved every inch of his flesh, leaving behind a bloody pulp of a man. Even after the disfiguring episode, my blood still screamed for more. I wanted to tear this town to pieces to bring Riley some peace.

"I will not be done until the Prizrak is beneath my feet."

"Vin." Massimo pressed his hand to my shoulder. "Go. Find Riley and lose yourself with her. The darkness is starting to take my brother from me." The pain was clear in his words. He had seen me at my worst, and now he was seeing it again.

"No. She doesn't want to see me."

"You don't know until you try."

Pushing him away, I fisted the blade in my palm. I glanced down at my bloodstained hand and sighed. Riley would be disappointed to know I was betraying my promise to her.

"Fine. I'll call her."

I stuffed the knife into my boot and headed toward the small office in the corner. If I was going to see her, I needed to wash away the sins first. My brothers and I kept extra clothes here in the event we got messy. After a quick shower, I sat down and dialed Riley. I needed to hear her voice—if she took my call. As I suspected, it went to voicemail.

"Riley. Please, Tesoro. Are you okay? How much longer are you going to stay away? I need to see you and know you are alright. I know I promised to give you space, but I don't know how much longer I can honor that." I ended the call and pocketed the phone.

The restaurant had suffered since her absence, and truth be told, I wasn't helping matters. After telling my brothers where I was headed, I climbed the basement stairs and slowly made my way to my motorcycle. I wanted to give her the space she needed, but my patience was wearing thin.

Halfway to her apartment, I changed my mind and pointed my bike in the direction of the restaurant—I wasn't ready to hear her end things.

I sat in my dark office, staring at the walls. I hadn't left the restaurant yet, and truthfully, I didn't want to. Since Riley had holed herself up in her apartment, I had avoided going home. My house felt empty without her there.

"I see you have been left all alone." The smooth Russian voice caused the hair on my neck to stand up. Dmitri Ivanov stepped from the shadows and smirked. "I hear you've been looking for me, Vincenzo… or should I say La Lama?"

I jumped from my perch and grabbed him. Dmitri sidestepped me, causing me to tumble into the hallway. He latched onto my jacket, dragging me to my feet.

"Why are you here?" All the rage I had felt over the last few days consumed me. "Why now, Dmitri? We've been hunting you."

"Yes. I've heard. I would have thought after sending your little lady a message to back off, you and your brothers would have listened. You haven't. I've come to tell you, if you don't stop meddling in Ivanov's affairs, the pretty girl will be next."

My hand moved of its own accord as my fingers wrapped around the steel blade buried in my boot.

"You're a brave man to come here alone."

"I'm not afraid of you. The FBI is breathing down your neck. La Lama is their biggest prize. If you fuck with me, you risk losing everything. You wouldn't take a chance on compromising the little agent you are tangled up with."

I closed my eyes and prayed for forgiveness for what I was about to do. Riley meant the world to me, but this monster would not rule over us any longer. The leather brushed against my knuckles as I slipped out my blade.

"You're wrong. I will watch as the Prizrak falls."

My blade buried itself in his tender gut. Dmitri's eyes widened with the realization of what I had done. I dragged his body out the back door and tossed him onto the ground.

"Riley means the world to me, which is exactly why removing you from this earth is the only thing to do. You'll never hurt my family again."

I gave myself over to the darkness as I took the life of a monster. Some say you trade your soul when you end the life of the Devil. Maybe that's true, but… it was worth it. I'd set fire to the ground, scorching the earth to save my family from the evil this man left in his wake. Riley may never forgive me, but at least this way I could protect her.

Dmitri Ivanov took his last strangled breath at the hands of another monster. At the sound of the last ragged breath he took, I looked down and stared at his crumpled form.

What had *I* done?

Staring down at my palms and the crimson coating them, I turned my head and heaved. It wasn't supposed to happen like this. I promised myself I wouldn't let my past catch up to my present. Yet as I stood in the alley behind my restaurant, standing over the lifeless man on the pavement, I knew it had. I thought nothing could be worse than the feeling I had in that moment.

I *was* wrong.

twenty

My mother was dead. I still couldn't comprehend the turn of events that occurred in the last month. I always knew going undercover would be risky. I just didn't realize to what extent. My heart had been torn into a thousand tiny pieces and tossed into the wind.

Fragments of who I was stared back at me as I stood in front of the mirror. Vincenzo had called every day since the funeral. I didn't answer, of course. Confusion plagued my thoughts as I washed up and pulled on some clothes. Between not eating, not sleeping, and avoiding the FBI and Vincenzo, I was worn for wear. Truth be told, I refused to admit what was wrong with me. I wasn't ready to accept what was happening.

Falling in love with the mob was not something I expected. And although Dmitri Ivanov had stolen something precious from me, I couldn't help but blame myself. My need for avenging my father's death had cost me my mother's. The worst part was I hadn't talked to my mother in years. She hated that I sought retribution for his murder and pleaded with me not to join the police force. Blinded by grief and rage, I ignored her.

A wave of dizziness had me gripping the sink. I felt like death warmed over, all due to stress and lack of sleep. I knew I needed to eat, but my stomach had been in knots since laying my mom to rest. My partner, Jackson, had come by multiple times to check on me. Turns out, he wasn't the dick I thought he was. Like Vincenzo, I told him to leave me alone. The department had given me extended time off, saying I needed to be one hundred percent before returning to my undercover position. They didn't want me to slip up and blow the operation. Little did they know I'd already fucked up more than I thought possible.

A knock at the front door startled me. I wasn't expecting anyone, so my hackles were raised. As I headed to the door, I grabbed my gun and held it down by my side. If someone intended to harm me, well, they better pray they got a shot off first. I peered out the peephole in disbelief at the person on the other side.

"Madison?" I pulled open the door and peeked around her into the hallway. "What are you doing here?"

"Can I come in?"

"Um…" I moved to the side and held my door open. "Yeah, of course."

"None of the men know I'm here,"—she brushed past me and stopped inside my apartment— "but I had to come and see if you were okay."

"Aren't you putting yourself at risk being here?"

"Risk for what? The FBI? I don't care about them. I care about you, Riley. I know it might be hard to believe, but I think of you as a friend. You brought that brooding brother-in-law-to-be of mine to life, and for that, I'll always care about you."

"I see." I ran my hand through my tangled hair to calm the tresses. "Would you like something to drink?"

"No, but can you tell me when the last time you ate something? You look like death."

"Thanks." I leaned against the counter and pressed my hands to my face.

"Riley, I've been where you are. I know what it's like to lose parents… maybe not so violently." She shuddered, thinking about her mother's untimely ending. "But what we feel is the same, nonetheless."

Madison had shared her past with me the night Ivanov delivered the box. I learned from an early age, she spent most of her life in foster care. I felt shameful the way I did.

"You're right. Losing a parent in any capacity is awful. I just feel guilty. I pushed her away because she wouldn't support my decision to be a cop—a decision that ultimately killed her."

"Stop." Madison raised an eyebrow and folded her arms across her chest. "This is not your fault. That monster Ivanov has wreaked havoc on all of us. When the Anastasis find him…" She took a breath. "Well, it won't be good."

"I just hope Vincenzo doesn't do anything stupid. My boss wants his head on a platter, and if he doesn't let me bring in Dmitri, I won't be able to protect him."

"You need to tell him that. But first,"—Madison slapped her hand on the counter— "you need a shower and food."

The mere mention of food made my stomach roll with disgust. I bolted past Madison, barely making it into the bathroom before I dry-heaved into the toilet.

"Um, Riley?" Madison stood at the door, her eyes on the counter wide with shock.

Pushing to my feet, I ignored her curious look. "I'm fine."

Madison started to speak. "I—"

"No. Leave it alone. Okay?" Madison pursed her lips and nodded. I knew it was killing her not to ask, but she simply helped me stand. She grabbed a washcloth and wet it down. Pressing it into my hand, she squeezed my shoulder.

"You know what this means, don't you?"

"Yes." I nodded. The truth had a way of finding itself out and when it did—it would change everything, and I wasn't ready for it. "I'll go see him tonight. Please don't say anything to anyone."

"I won't. He's holed up at the restaurant, you know." I nodded. Her message was clear. Madison started toward the front door and paused. "I'm here for you if you need anything. You can call me anytime, no matter what, okay?"

"Thank you."

Closing the door behind her, I pressed my head against it and sighed. Everything was falling apart around me. All I could do was pray Vincenzo wouldn't do anything dumb. I didn't know if I could protect us both if he did.

Deciding it was time to face him, I grabbed my keys and headed to Bellissimo's.

"VINCENZO?" MY VOICE ECHOED OFF THE DUMPSTER.

"Go back inside." He lowered his head, staring at the blood pooling around his shoes. His hand was still wrapped around the blade he'd obviously just buried into the man lying inches away from his feet.

"You know I can't do that, Vin." I swallowed down the bile threatening to spill.

"Yes, you can. Turn around and walk through that door."

I took a deep breath and closed my eyes. "I'm sorry, I can't."

"Goddamn it! Please. If you really love me like you say you do, you'll turn around and leave me to deal with this."

"You know why I can't walk away." The tears threatened to fall as I stepped toward him. "Don't make me choose."

"Seems like you've already done that." He dropped the heavy metal to the ground, the sound echoing through the alleyway. "Can you at least call my brothers first?"

"It didn't have to come to this. There was another way, Vincenzo."

"Another way? This piece of shit tried to ruin my life. He tried to have my sister kidnapped. Then,"—he took a breath — "he nearly killed Antonio. There wasn't another way. You know as well as I do, he would have walked if the police were involved. He was too powerful."

"And now what? He's dead, and you'll be a martyr in jail. You say if I loved you, I'll walk back inside. What about you?" My voice cracked with desperation.

"What about me?" he snapped.

"If you loved me, you wouldn't have let it come to this." I shook my head, tears finally burning a trail down my skin.

"Sometimes, we have to decide what path to take. This is the path I chose. My family means everything to me. *Everything*!" He balled his fists against his thighs. "I thought you realized that by now."

"I told you I wouldn't walk this path with you. I can't. Your family means too much to you. Well, so does mine. It just looks a little different from yours."

"Family? You think your so-called family is going to stand beside you when they learn you've been *fucking* the enemy?" His voice was laced with venom as he turned to face me. His face was a mask of rage, making me suck in a breath.

I stiffened at his sudden change in demeanor. "Fuck you, Vincenzo."

"Just do what you have to. This road was going to lead here at some point. We both knew we couldn't last." He brushed past me, pausing beside my ear. "But never forget my words, il mio Tesoro. When I was buried inside that pussy of yours, I meant every word I said. I *love* you. I'm sorry it has come to this. I'll be waiting inside."

I couldn't stop the sharp intake of breath as he pushed inside, leaving me alone in the dark. I was torn between doing the right thing and my love for him.

Deep down, I knew it would come to this. He hadn't been wrong in saying our path only had one destination—he was right. Only the path was one that led to an *end.*

I felt sick to my stomach as I took in the bloody man in front of me. Truth be told, Dmitri Ivanov deserved everything he'd gotten. As I stared back at the closed door, I knew I had been wrong when I said my family looked different. *He* was my family, not the FBI. Dmitri had taken my mother from me, and this… this was Vincenzo's way of protecting me. I tugged my cell phone from my pocket and called the one person who could help me. She answered immediately.

"Hello."

"Remember when you said you would help me if I needed it?"

Madison replied without hesitation. "Yes."

"Massimo needs to come get Vincenzo from the restaurant. I can stall the FBI long enough for him to take Vincenzo from here."

"Riley, what's happened?" Madison's voice was a whisper.

"Dmitri Ivanov is dead."

"What?" She sounded as shocked as I felt.

"All you need to know is he's dead. If Vincenzo's here when the police show up, I wouldn't be able to protect him. Do you understand what I'm saying? Madison, he isn't going to leave willingly. That's why you need to convince Massimo to come and take him."

She was silent for a moment, but I knew she understood what was at risk.

"Yes. I understand."

I shoved the phone in my pocket and waited. Vincenzo would not like what I was about to do, but it was the only way. He'd made his decision—now I was making mine. Staring at the dead form lying in the dark alley for what felt like hours, I jumped when someone spoke behind me.

"Riley." Donny's voice reverberated off the dumpster, snapping me from the trance I was in.

I bent down and picked up Vincenzo's knife.

"Donny."

He watched in shock as I wiped the blade handle on my shirt.

"What are you doing?"

"What needs to be done?" I twirled the blade in my palm. "You need to get him out of here. He can't be here when I call this in."

Donnie looked at the knife, staring at it in confusion. "We can get rid of the body."

"No, you can't... not this time. The Feds have been waiting to catch this man for a decade. If he vanishes, the suspicion will be back on Vincenzo. This must be called in."

"He'll go to jail, Riley."

"No." I shook my head. "He won't. Just trust me, okay?"

The door opened to reveal Massimo and Antonio. They stared at my bloodstained shirt and crimson-stained hands.

"Riley?" Antonio stepped forward and reached out to take the knife.

"No." I jerked my hand back. "It has to be this way."

"Your prints are all over that blade. You're going to implicate yourself. Just hand it over."

"I can't. You need to leave. All of you. If my plan is going to work, you can't be here when they come. Please." Hot tears fell freely as I pleaded with the men surrounding me.

Antonio glanced at Massimo. "He won't like this."

"I don't care. He did this because I asked him to. I won't have him in jail. Please. Just go. Take him as far away as you can. I don't need him fucking this up."

"Are you sure about this, Riley?" Massimo's eyes held part respect and part worry.

"Yes. Please go."

"Brother." Antonio held his hand out. "Vincenzo won't forgive us if we let her do what I think she's about to do."

"It's not our decision." Massimo tipped his head. "We won't walk away from you, Riley. This makes you family. Come, Antonio. We need to muscle Vin out of here. Donny, we'll need you, too. Let's go." He paused. "I'll text you when it's done."

I waited until they left me in the alley alone before slipping my phone out again. As soon as Massimo's text came in, my thumb hovered over the call button. Once I did this, there was no going back. I'd be turning my back on my oath… on the FBI, but the dead man at my feet left little room for options. He'd led me to this moment. He'd driven these people mad with vengeance—hell, he'd sent me crazy with it as well. I pressed my hand to my stomach and took a deep breath.

"Lawson. I didn't expect to hear from you."

My voice was cold as I spoke the words I knew I could never get back.

"Something's happened, Jackson. I need you to bring a crime scene van and the coroner to Bellissimo."

"What the fuck? Vincenzo finally slipped up?"

"No, he didn't." I swallowed the burning acid in my esophagus. "I did."

"What are you talking about?"

"Look, just get here, okay? I haven't called the Anastasis or Vincenzo. They don't know what's going on yet."

"Don't know what? You're not making any sense, Riley. If Vincenzo didn't do something, why do you need the crime unit and coroner?"

"Because…" I took a deep breath. "I killed Dmitri Ivanov."

twenty-one

VINCENZO

"WHY ARE we going to Italy? Won't it appear like I'm fleeing the country? This won't help me when I am arrested."

Massimo and Antonio settled in their seats as the plane taxied down the runway, about to lift off.

My nerves coiled in my gut. I had just killed Dmitri Ivanov, leaving his bloody body in the alley behind my restaurant. Not to mention the woman I loved, an FBI agent, was the one who'd found me.

Massimo glanced at Antonio and nodded.

"Now that you can't jump off the plane, I think I should tell you what's going on. But before I do, I need your word that you're not going to lose your shit. We have a long flight, and I don't need you going berserker on me mid-flight." I nodded for him to continue. "Riley has a plan to keep you from being implicated in his murder."

I leaned forward in my seat, looking between my brothers. "I don't understand."

My brother closed his eyes and sighed.

"I don't quite understand myself, Vin. All I know is she called Madison and asked that we come and get you. She only told us that having you gone would help her plan."

My fingers dug into the edge of the armrest as I shifted my body, trying to get comfortable. But the anxiety I was feeling rose to ten decibels.

"Give me my phone."

"What are you going to do? You can't call her while we're in the air, Vincenzo." Antonio crossed his leg over his knee and leaned back against the seat. "Do you trust her?"

"Yes," I answered without hesitation.

As strange as it seemed, I trusted her. I knew she had been at war with herself when I left her standing over Dmitri Ivanov's body. Her body language told me she wanted to turn and pretend she hadn't seen what I'd done, but her heart was conflicted. She was the FBI. How was she supposed to leave and pretend I hadn't just killed a man?

She couldn't.

And I didn't expect her to. I'd known our time together would likely end. We were from two different worlds—even if I desperately wanted to pretend we weren't.

"Then you have to trust she knows what she's doing."

"I don't like this. Why didn't she tell me what she had planned? I could have helped her."

"No, Vin, you couldn't have. I know you, and so does she, apparently. She knew, whatever she was planning to do, you wouldn't like it. So, she needed to remove you from the equation."

"This is bullshit." I pressed my head to the back of the headrest and closed my eyes. Even though I trusted her, something was wrong. The only way to keep me from being implicated was if she framed someone else, but that would be nearly impossible. Unless…

"Mother fucker." I bolted upright and glared at my brother. "She's going to say it was her, isn't she?" When Massimo refused to meet my gaze, I knew I was right. "Turn this plane around, Massimo. *Now*." I tried to stand, but Massimo pushed me back down.

"Calm down. We don't know if that's what she's planning."

"It is. There's no other explanation. She'll have to say someone did it, and who is that going to be? Tell me. Who do you think that is?"

The realization spread across Massimo's features as the reality of my words set in.

"Why would she do something like that?" He glanced at Antonio, who just shrugged. "It would be career suicide, not to mention she would be arrested for murder."

"I don't know." I tugged at my hair in frustration. "But in my gut, I know that's what she is planning."

"Maybe not, Brother." Antonio pressed his hand to my knee. "Let's land, then we can find out what's going on. Madison stayed behind to make it less suspicious. It's not unusual for us to go to Italy, and only the pilot knows when we left. To the world, we are already there and have been for days."

"I fucked up. I dragged her into this mess… This is my fault."

"No. It's Dmitri Ivanov's fault. You know as well as I do, he was there to kill you. I would have done the same thing."

My mind whirled with a myriad of thoughts. I wish Riley had simply arrested me. I belonged behind bars for the horrific things I had done, and not just in the last twenty-four hours. Everything I touched turned to darkness, and now, I had ruined the one thing that meant more than the breath I took.

twenty-two

RILEY

THE LIGHTS FLASHED, filling the alley with an eerie barrage of colors. I watched in fascination as my team… well, former team, filled the narrow space. The pavement was covered in red and lined with yellow tape. Even the smell filling the air spoke of death.

Death of a *man*.

Death of my *career*.

"Riley." Jackson's voice called out, forcing me back to the present. "I need you to tell me what happened here. How is it Dmitri Ivanov was even here?"

"He came to kill Vincenzo, but he's in Italy with his brothers." His body was covered with a sheet, but I couldn't take my eyes off him. "I was here, just closing up."

"Okay… what happened?"

Bile rose in my gut, I leaned over and wretched, spilling the contents of my stomach on the street. Wiping my mouth with the back of my hand, I closed my eyes and continued talking, the lies rolling off my tongue.

"I heard a noise at the backdoor. I came outside to see what and was surprised to find Dmitri leaning against the brick wall. He was waiting for Vincenzo."

"Did he threaten you?"

"No. He threatened Vincenzo. Said he was here to speak with my boss and demanded to know where he was." The lie kept rolling off my tongue with such ease I didn't recognize myself. "I told him Italy, but he didn't care. He was so full of rage and hate."

"Why did you stab him, Riley?"

"I don't know. I just saw red. This man was responsible for my pare… my dad's death." I caught myself before slipping up that he had been the reason my mother was dead. To the police and my team, my mom had died in a car accident. "I couldn't let him continue. He tried to grab me, but…" I swallowed and pressed my eyes closed. This was the moment I wouldn't be able to take back. I pressed my hand to my belly and took a breath. "I stabbed him. I killed Dmitri Ivanov."

"You know, this isn't how I wanted things to happen." Jackson shook his head. His shoulders slumped as he reached out to grab my arm. He pulled out his handcuffs. "But I have to place you in custody and take your badge. At least until the investigation is over."

I knew I had to take the burden on myself. It was the only way to protect Vincenzo and the secret I was hiding.

"Is there anything else you need to tell me?"

I looked down at my feet through the tears rolling down my cheeks.

"I was involved with Vincenzo."

Jackson stiffened. "What do you mean, involved?"

"Exactly as it sounds. I got in too deep, and we became… intimate."

"Jesus Christ, Riley. Do you know what you've done?"

"Yes." I could vividly hear the last nail being hammered into my coffin. "That's why I'm telling you. It will come out and destroy any hope of making this disappear."

"Fuck." Jackson eased me into the back of his car and slammed the door.

I watched as he walked over to my superior. I could see him speaking, his body stiff with anger. Pritz's eyes bored into mine with a look of disappointment and disgust. He shook his head and said something to Jackson, making him turn back to look at me. The shame for me both men held in their eyes stabbed me straight through my core. Both my parents were dead and gone. Vincenzo had to stay away to protect his family, leaving me truly alone. I was surprised when Madison burst through the back door. She was screaming at someone close to the dead body. I watched in amazement as she approached Jackson and Pritz. Her anger was palpable, even in the alleyway.

Jackson nodded and led her to the car. "You can have a minute with her. I'll be here listening."

"Riley." Madison grabbed my hand. "When I said I would do anything for you, I didn't mean this. What were you thinking?"

"I had to end this. Now,"—I blinked away tears and turned my head to look out the opposite window— "Vincenzo can be free."

"Free?" Madison scoffed and glanced briefly over her shoulder at the scene. "Do you think he'll be okay with this? He loves you, Riley. Despite the lies, he chose you, and what about—"

My head snapped to look at her and I cut off her words. "Don't."

"You're being stupid. They'll find out soon enough what you're hiding. Then what? How do you think Vin will react?"

"I don't know. I just need some time to get through this."

"I hope you know what you're doing." Madison shook her head. "You could spend the rest of your life in jail, Riley."

"That's a chance I'll take."

"And what about?" She motioned her hand toward me.

"I know Vincenzo will be there when the time comes. Please. I have to do this. Don't let him try to stop me, or we'll both end up in jail."

"Ma'am." Jackson pressed his hand to the open door. "I'm afraid I have to take her to headquarters now. Are the Anastasis coming home?"

"They are wrapping up business in Italy, and Vincenzo and my fiancé cannot get away. Antonio Anastasi will be back tomorrow."

Jackson narrowed his eyes. "A murder occurred at Vincenzo's restaurant, and he isn't coming back?"

"That's not what I said. Don't put words in my mouth. Trust me, he wants to be here, but family business doesn't stop for murder. Antonio will be here tomorrow. He and I will be in touch with our family attorney's information."

"Why would the Anastasi family attorney get involved?"

"Riley is one of us. We will take care of her legal fees and anything else she may need. Any other questions, *Agent* Jackson?" Madison cocked an eyebrow at him. "Now, Riley, you know the drill. Say nothing until our attorney is present. I've already called him, and he's sending over one of the partners. You said you're taking her to headquarters? What's the address?"

I nodded at Madison as Jackson closed the door, shutting me off from the world again. I looked down at my hands clasped in front of me, wearing silver bracelets I never thought I would see. My heart thumped against my chest, threatening to break out. I hoped I was doing the right thing. If I was wrong in my plan, then everything would be for nothing, and everyone would suffer.

I pressed my palms against my stomach—this was no longer just about me.

twenty-three

VINCENZO

I PACED THE VERANDA, staring out into the beautiful countryside. "When are we heading back?" The cerulean blue water lapped against the rocky seaside as the waves greeted the shore. The lush green trees lined the coast, welcoming anyone who ventured into the country. Italy usually had a way of making you forget about your worries, but not today. It had been a week since I was forced on a plane and dragged to my parent's house in Sicily. Antonio had stayed on the plane to return to Vegas—as part of the plan.

The *plan*.

I scoffed at the mere thought of what she'd done. Riley had confessed to a crime I'd committed.

"Tonight."

"Fine." I scrubbed my palm down my face. My beard had become an unruly monster on my skin, threatening to bury me in sorrow. I wasn't sleeping or eating—my head wouldn't turn off after learning what Riley had done. The worse part was I could tell they were keeping something from me. "What did Antonio say?"

"Well…" Massimo pushed off the railing and downed his drink. "The attorney said he was sure she would be found not guilty, but the Feds are pushing this to trial. Because she admitted to being involved with you, there is suspicion self-defense wasn't the motive for stabbing him."

"It wasn't." I ground my teeth together. "You know that. How the fuck did it come to this, and what aren't you telling me?"

"What do you mean?"

"I know you're hiding something." I folded my arms across my chest. "I can tell."

"You're delusional, Vin. When was the last time you slept or ate? Hell, you look like a homeless man."

I threw my glass into the yard and slammed my hands against the wood.

"Don't lie to me."

"You should tell him." My mother's voice caused me to turn around. She was standing in the doorway watching us.

"Mama," Massimo growled.

"No. He has a right to know."

I stiffened at her words. "Know what?"

"Fuck." Massimo turned away from me and glanced out into the lush foliage. "I can't, Mama. It's not our place to tell him. It's hers."

"Tell me what?" I stepped toward him with my fists balled. "Someone better talk."

"Just know Riley believed she was doing this for you. She was trying to protect you, and herself, if I had to bet." My mother stepped onto the veranda. "Women do risky things for the people they love, Vincenzo. Remember that. *Promise* me." Her eyes held pain as she waited for me to answer.

"I promise." I looked into my brother's eyes. The expression staring back was filled with angst. "Massimo?"

"Please don't make me betray Madison. I promised her I wouldn't say anything. Talk to Riley."

"Talk to Riley? How, Fratello? She sits in a jail cell, awaiting a trial that will probably take months. The judge denied bond because of her ties to us, making her a possible flight risk."

"Please," Massimo begged again, his voice cracking with the turmoil of having to choose between me and the woman he loved.

"Fine. I'll ask Madison myself."

"Good luck with that."

I stormed past my brother and into the house.

If we were leaving tonight, I needed to clean myself up. If Madison wouldn't tell me what they were hiding, my only option was to see Riley. I wasn't sure if I could keep myself from confessing when I saw her, and that scared me. If I told them I was the one who stabbed him, then we would both go to jail. I was torn about what to do. Somehow, Riley had broken through my blackened heart and breathed life back into it. Falling in love with her had been unexpected.

Even after I found out who she really was, I couldn't stop the way I felt. She'd become mine. Riley was the air I breathed— my very reason for existing. She was the reason I had not yet given into the darkness that threatened to take me. Her loyalty to me and my family spoke volumes. One thing was certain… I wouldn't stop until she was free. I didn't care what I had to do—even if it meant getting my hands dirty *again*.

I stormed into the bathroom and braced my hands against the sink. Lost to a million thoughts running through my head, I didn't hear my grandmother come in.

"Vincenzo." She held her head high. "Come. We talk."

Pushing off the porcelain edge, I stalked into the bedroom and sat down beside the one woman who could give me an ass chewing, aside from my mother.

"Nonna, I take you've heard of what I've done?"

She pressed her palm to my knee. "Look at me, dolche bambino."

Her sweet sentiment caused me to close my eyes in shame. I didn't deserve to be called sweet anything.

"I've known for a long time what your role in the family was." Her Italian words washed over me. "It is part of who we are. I only hate it's caused you pain along the way. But if what Massimo tells me is true… this woman deserves to be by your side."

My head shot up to look at her. "What do you mean? You know what they're keeping from me, don't you?"

She nodded. "But it is her secret to tell Vincenzo. And when she does, how you respond will prove if this love is real or not. Women like Riley don't come around often. Massimo was lucky to find his heart… now it's your turn. But I warn you." She stood, pausing in front of me. "You are the only thing that can dismantle the future you're worthy of. Don't be a fool and let anger cloud your vision."

I stood and pulled her into my arms. "I love you, Nonna."

"And I you. Now," she pulled open the door. "Go get the girl."

THE CELL WAS cold and dank. To be honest, it smelled worse than anything I could have imagined. Of course, my current predicament didn't help. I couldn't hold down the food they were trying to pass off as edible. I leaned my head against the foam pillow and closed my eyes, thankful my parents weren't around to see me like this.

"Riley Lawson, you have a visitor."

I sat up, the blood rushing to my head, causing a moment of dizziness.

"A visitor?" I squeaked out.

The guard slid open the cell door. The metal creaking and slamming as he snatched it open. "Yes." His face soured as I stood and started toward him.

"But my attorney wasn't due back until tomorrow."

"It's not your attorney. Mr. Anastasi is here to see you." He sneered in disgust as he grabbed my arm and tugged me into the hallway.

My heart began beating erratically inside my chest. "Oh." Surely Vincenzo wasn't stupid enough to risk coming here. The Feds still believed he had a role in what happened and would watch his every move.

The guard placed the cuffs on my hands, and I followed him toward the tiny room. A chair was placed in front of a plexiglass window, and a tiny phone receiver hung next to it. The sight of it mocked me from the doorway. Taking a deep breath, I stepped behind the chair. Vincenzo was seated on the opposite side of the glass, his eyes boring into me. He picked up the phone on his side and pressed it to his face, his eyes never leaving mine. The guard removed the cuffs as he sealed me inside, the locking mechanism causing me to jump. I lowered myself into the chair and lifted the receiver.

"Riley."

His deep voice ricocheted through my entire being, sending a chill through my veins. There was no way I could hide my emotions as I fought back the tears threatening to spill.

"Vincenzo." My voice cracked with emotion. "Why are you here?"

"You know why, Riley. Why did you do this?"

My eyes cut to the guard, who was watching us with intent. Every word was being measured and recorded. If he said something that gave off even the slightest hint he knew what I had done, everything I'd worked for would be lost.

"I had to. I couldn't let him destroy any more people."

Vincenzo rubbed his face and sighed. "What aren't you telling me? Madison and Massimo won't tell me what you're hiding."

"What do you mean?"

"*Riley*." His commanding tone sent shivers down my spine.

He knew—I don't know how, but he did. I knew once I breathed it into life, everything would change, but I couldn't continue to carry this alone. Soon, everyone would know my secret, and that's not how I wanted him to find out.

"Before I tell you, promise me you won't do anything stupid. Michael is confident we can win this… I just have to ride out my time here until the trial."

"Michael?" Vincenzo pressed his elbows against the table.

"Michael Brighton. My attorney. He works for Don Giuliani, your family's legal counsel."

"I see." He nodded.

"No, Vin. I need to hear you say it. Promise me you'll let him deal with this and you won't do anything stupid." I closed my eyes and sent a prayer to the heavens.

"I promise," he forced out.

"This isn't just about you or me anymore, Vin. I had to take care of Dmitri and get him out of our life forever. He just made it easy by threatening me."

His eyebrow quirked at my lie, and I swear I saw a moment where he considered outing me right there, but he must have seen the desperation in my expression. He pinched the bridge of his nose and sighed.

"Then why are you sitting behind bars? And why tell them we were involved? If you hadn't, you would be out right now."

"I know, but eventually, they would have found out we were together. I couldn't lie about it. It was better I told them now because I wouldn't be able to hide it much longer."

"After this was over, it wouldn't matter." He shook his head.

"There would be no way to hide our relationship before this case is over."

He leaned forward, trying to get a better look at me. "I don't understand."

"I didn't mean for this to happen." I pressed my hand to the glass. "I love you Vincenzo, remember that."

He pressed his palm to the glass against mine. My heart stuttered when his voice cracked with desperation, and he dropped his head in defeat.

"Just tell me, Riley. *Please*."

"I had to tell them about us." I swallowed down the vomit threatening to force its way out. "Because hiding a baby will be nearly impossible in a few months."

Vincenzo's head snapped up, his eyes locking on mine. The shock in his eyes drew me in, trapping me there. I watched as a lone tear trickled down his cheek and spilled onto the Formica countertop. His palm pressed against the barrier as he leaned in closer, as though it would allow him to hear me more clearly. I kept my hand there, the cool plexiglass separating our touch, and squeezed my eyes closed.

"What did you say?" His voice was constricted as he searched my gaze for the truth.

"I'm pregnant." I forced out the words through a throat that felt as if I'd swallowed glass.

Everything came to a standstill at that moment. Vincenzo couldn't turn away from me, both of us overwhelmed with emotion as our tears fell. I didn't move or speak. My hand remained pressed against his through the barrier. It was as if I was trying to feel his skin beneath mine. I glanced over at the guard, who looked as shocked by my words as he was.

"When?" he breathed into the phone. His hand dropped to his side.

"When, what?" I curled my fingers in, clutching my hands in front of me.

"When did you know?"

Taking a deep breath, I forced out the truth. "A while now. It's why I did what I did. I couldn't risk losing you."

"You're pregnant with my child, Riley. Didn't you think I should have a say in your fucking plan?" His hand slammed down on the table, making me jump.

"Vincenzo," I hissed, glancing back at the uniformed man who'd taken a step toward us. "Please."

He glanced over at the guard and clicked his teeth. He was pissed, and rightfully so. Had he known about the child I was carrying, he'd have never let me do this. He would have demanded I walk away and let him take care of Dmitri. But that would have put him here, and I'd be left raising our baby alone. At least this way, I had a chance at freedom. They would have figured out how to throw the book at him, no questions asked.

"Does anyone else know?"

I knew my answer would cause him pain. "Only Madison and your brother."

"Why haven't you told the attorney?"

I wasn't sure how to answer him. Once I spoke the words out loud to someone—the FBI would know my secret. It wasn't as though I was intentionally trying to hide it from them. I just wasn't ready to deal with the shit storm that would follow. "I don't know. I guess I was scared."

"This *changes* everything. Didn't you stop to think the judge would have sympathy and let you out on bond, for fuck's sake?" Vincenzo was seething mad. He paced the tiny room like a feral cat.

"No."

"I'm calling the attorney as soon as I leave. He needs to know this additional information. Goddamn it, Riley. You didn't need to fix this on your own. I could have helped you."

"Please don't hate me." The flood gates opened, and the tears fell like hot embers across my face.

He rushed to the glass and pressed his hand against the barrier again.

"Hate you? I could never hate you. I hate myself, Riley. It's my fault you're sitting behind bars. *Mine*. Do you understand that? If I hadn't gotten you into this fucking mess…" I watched as he fisted his hair and his eyelids scrunched closed as if to seal off the demons hiding behind his eyes. "It doesn't matter. I'm going to fix this, Riley. I promise you."

"Times up."

The guard opened the door to my tiny visitation room and stepped toward me. I held my hands out for him to cuff me before walking back to my cell.

"Please, Vincenzo. You have to know this was the only way."

"I won't accept that." He pinned me with a serious look. "However, I will respect your wishes. But"—his eyes zeroed in on the shiny metal wrapped around my delicate skin, and he clenched his jaw— "I will get you out of here."

"I love you," I whispered, knowing he likely couldn't hear the muffled sentiment through the glass window.

To my shock, his eyes found mine, and I watched as he mouthed the words back to me before disappearing out the door.

"You're pregnant with that scum's baby?" the guard grunted as he jerked me toward my cell.

"You know nothing of that man's true character—only what you've been told. Mind your fucking business and loosen your grip or I will report you for inmate abuse."

His fingers loosened from around my arm. "I don't care what you think, Lady. That man is a criminal and should be behind bars, just like you."

"Fuck you." He shoved me inside my cell, causing me to fall to my knees.

"Watch your mouth inmate, or I'll have you thrown in solitary for your attitude." He slammed the bars shut, locking me in my coffin.

My palms pressed to the hard cement as I tried to push up. Overwhelmed by everything, I gave in to the emotions I had been fighting back and collapsed onto the hard concrete floor. Feelings of loneliness and fear consumed me. What had I done?

If my attorney couldn't get me off the charges, I would give birth to my baby in prison. I slid to my side and curled into a fetal position.

"I'm sorry."

My voice echoed into the emptiness as I let myself cry for the things I'd lost.

twenty-five

VINCENZO

My EARS FILLED with a rushing sound as the blood poured through my veins. Every nerve was firing on overdrive as the words she spoke sunk in.

Pregnant.

I was going to be a dad, yet… the woman I loved and was carrying my baby was locked up for my sins. I had just slipped my phone from my pocket to call our family attorney when I heard my name.

"Mr. Anastasi."

Glancing up from the device, I took in the man standing in front of me. From the looks of his cheap suit and two-dollar haircut, I guessed he was an agent.

"What?"

"I'm Agent Mitchell." Taking a step toward me, he thrust his hand out. "Jackson's new partner. Mind if we chat a moment?"

I should have known someone would call the Feds and tell them I was here. "Yes, I mind. What is there to talk about?"

"How about the fact your known rival was found dead at your restaurant, and that *woman* in there is taking the fall?"

I gripped his shirt and pushed him against the wall.

"Let me tell you something. That woman is not taking the fall for anyone. She acted in self-defense, and your department knows it. You've just got a hard-on for my family, so you're too blind to see it."

"I think you should let me go before I throw you in jail for assaulting a federal agent."

I let out the breath I was holding and glanced around the room. We were being watched by a dozen men in uniform. Going to jail right now was the last thing I needed. Right now, the only thing important was telling our attorney the news.

"Now." He straightened his shirt and grinned. "How about that chat?"

Fuck. I walked right into his trap. There was no other choice but to comply and give him five minutes.

"Fine." I followed him to a small interrogation room and sat down. Pulling my phone out, I pressed record and set it on the table.

"Is there a reason you feel the need to record this, Mr. Anastasi?"

"I don't trust you or your men watching from behind that glass wall. You could use my words against me, so having them recorded protects me. I am here without representation, after all." I leaned back in the hard chair and folded my arms across my chest. Holding his gaze, I grinned. "Can we get started? I have business to attend to."

"Speaking about business. How is it a man can be murdered in your building, a woman who you're romantically involved with charged for the crime, and you don't come back immediately?"

"My family's business is not on trial here, but I will give you this. I was wrapped up in a negotiation that would not lend to my disappearance. My brother flew back immediately to aid in her release, and I came back as soon as I could. It killed me to be in Italy knowing the woman I love is stuck in this hellhole."

He flinched slightly at the open admission of my feelings for Riley. "Right. Can you tell me why Dmitri Ivanov was there hunting you down?"

"As you know, there has been a long-standing rivalry between the Italians and Russians. Not long ago, Dmitri approached us about a business deal. We turned him down, and he didn't take too kindly to that."

"Why did you turn him down? Isn't his business something your family would typically dabble in?"

"No." I laughed at his obvious attempt to confuse me into implicating my family for illegal business. That wouldn't happen—*ever*. "My family doesn't partake in anything illegal. We've worked too hard to get where we are, and dealing with slime like him would eventually bring us down."

"Didn't he kidnap your brother?"

I tried to hide my shock. No one was supposed to know that outside the family.

"No, he didn't. Antonio was involved in a hiking accident in Chile."

"That's not the information we got." He wrote something down in his notebook.

"Well, it's wrong. Would you like me to give you the number of a friend who was with him?" I knew I was risking myself and the family by doing this without talking to Matias first, but deep down, I knew he would cover for us.

"That would be great."

"I have somewhere to be, and since you aren't arresting me, Agent Mitchell, I think this conversation is done." I stood and grabbed my phone. "You'll be hearing from my attorney. Miss Lawson will not be held here much longer."

Agent Mitchell followed me out the door. "That number, Mr. Anastasi?"

I paused, turning to look over my shoulder. "My attorney will send it along with Riley's release order."

I could feel all eyes on me as I passed the front counter. The place was a cesspool, and there was no way I was going to allow Riley to stay here another minute. Pressing my phone to my ear, I took a deep breath.

"Massimo, call the attorney and Antonio. Have them meet us at the club. There's something we need to discuss."

He paused before answering me. "I assume she told you?"

"Yes, and we will not stop until Riley has been released. I will not have her sitting in jail pregnant with my child."

I pocketed the device in my pants and straddled my bike. Giving the jail one last glance, I smiled at Agent Mitchell, who was still watching me from the top of the steps. I tugged my helmet on and revved the engine. He thought he would corner me into lying. They had no idea who they were dealing with. I'd do whatever was necessary to free her. Nothing—and I mean *nothing*—he could do would keep me from saving the woman I loved.

I made it to Discoteca in record time and wasn't surprised to find everyone there. Madison rushed to my side, throwing her arms around me, and letting out a sob.

"I'm so sorry, Vin. I wanted to tell you, but I promised her I wouldn't."

"Madison." I leaned her away from my body, gripping her shoulders. "I'm not mad at you. You're a good friend, and I'm grateful you were there for her when I couldn't be."

"You're not mad?" She smiled at me, swiping at her tears.

Shaking my head, I pulled her into another hug. "No, Maddie, I'm not"

"Get your hands off my woman." Massimo slapped my shoulder, tugging her into his arms. "We're going to get yours out so you can keep your paws off this one."

I followed Massimo to his office, where Michael was waiting.

Antonio's phone rang behind me. He glanced down at the screen.

"Excuse me. I need to take this."

Ignoring his sudden departure, I turned to the attorney.

"Mr. Brighton, I want her out tonight."

He palmed the back of his neck and blew out a frustrated breath.

"First, call me Michael. We're going to be working close over the next few weeks. Second, they aren't going to let her out. I'm sorry Mr. Anastasi. The partners and I have been on the phone since you left the jail."

"Why not?" I slammed my hands down on the table, rattling the glasses and spilling out some of their contents.

"They said pregnant women have been in jail before, and she's not any different. They worry we will hustle her off to Italy where they can't find her."

"Fuck." I picked up my glass and downed what was left of the bourbon. "Who is this new prosecutor I hear is going to try the case?"

"She was hired a few weeks ago. Some new hotshot out of New York. They're concerned we have people in our pocket." Michael slipped off his coat and tossed it over a chair. Young but sharp, he was the newest member of Don Giuliani's team. I know Don had vetted and knew he would fit in with the family's team of attorneys—even though he was young.

"Great," I grumbled beneath my breath.

Antonio stepped into the room and searched the faces standing around. His body went rigid when his eyes landed on the attorney.

"Michael."

"Antonio."

The tension was obvious between the two men as they stared each other down like they were in a Mexican standoff.

"Is there a problem here?" Massimo glared at them.

"No." Antonio shoved inside and plopped down on a chair.

"Good. Can we discuss this new prosecutor? There has to be a way to get her on our side."

Massimo handed me a fresh drink before sitting down. "Donny, what dirt were you able to dig up on her?"

"Well," he pushed off the wall and tossed a folder onto the table. "At twenty-eight, she's the youngest female hired as a criminal prosecutor. She fast tracked herself through school and made a name for herself in New York. She's known for being one of the most ruthless prosecutors around and never losing a case. She was suggested to the Las Vegas prosecutor's office by the Feds. As Michael stated, they were concerned we would have the others on our payroll. Her parents died some time ago. They were in the Twin Towers when they came down. Her only surviving relative is a brother in Reno."

"Damn. That sucks about her parents. What was her name again?" Antonio asked, watching Michael the entire time.

I wondered if there was something they weren't telling us.

"Rachel Hill."

I rubbed my temples. "This doesn't help us get Riley out of jail."

"Well… I have some good news on that front." Michael smiled, glancing at his phone. "I just received word Miss Hill convinced the judge who denied bond to change her mind. She feels Riley's not a flight risk and considering her condition, should be let out on bond."

"Seriously?" I stood. "When can I get her?"

"She will be released tomorrow evening, after her paperwork is processed and she's placed into your custody. But I must warn you…" He took a breath. "I believe there is an ulterior motive. I think the Feds are hoping for you two to slip up and give them the evidence they need to convict her. So letting her out is a ploy."

"That's not what we need. Vin, are you sure it's wise for her to stay with you? Perhaps she should stay with Antonio."

"No, she'll stay with me. I don't give a fuck about the FBI, or anyone else, for that matter. Knowing the prosecutor is looking for a fuck up doesn't bode well for us, regardless of where she stays."

"No, it doesn't,"—Antonio smiled, pushing the folder on the desk toward me— "but I have an idea to fix that."

"How the hell do you plan to do that?" I snapped, my patience running thin.

"Rumor has it she is in the market for a contractor. I plan on working for the man she hired. Once I'm in, I'll see what I can learn about her and get her under our thumb."

"How much did that cost us?"

"Nothing. The man she hired is one of Miguel's."

I shook my head and chuckled. "Wow."

"Yep." Antonio leaned back into his chair and propped his feet on the table. "I start this weekend."

"Move fast. The longer it takes, the longer my pregnant wife must deal with the stress—stress I caused her."

"Wife?" Massimo raised a brow. "Um, Vincenzo. I hate to be the bearer of bad news, but you aren't married."

"Not yet, but as soon as we can get her out on bail, I plan to make her mine—permanently."

THE SOUND of the metal bars rattling woke me from my restless sleep. Every sound inside the jail kept me on edge, and I felt as though I hadn't slept in ages. Being on this side of the law was eye-opening.

"Wake up." the guard grunted as he stepped inside my cell. "Looks like you were granted bail and your piece of shit boyfriend posted the money."

I rubbed my temples and closed my eyes. Somehow, Vincenzo had managed exactly what he'd promised. And now I was going home even if I was still labeled a criminal. Being charged with murder hadn't been a shock. However, only the attorney and I knew the entire story—not even the Anastasis had been told of the tiny detail keeping me under suspicion's eye. Tiny… that's an understatement. When Michael had gotten the autopsy report, I begged him to hold off on telling the family what he'd learned. I wanted to be the one to spill the shocking news. Hell, I was still distressed by the revelation myself.

The walk down the corridor toward my freedom felt longer than it was. I had changed into the clothes Vincenzo brought for me. My other clothes were locked up in evidence, and he didn't want me to have to stay in my prisoner uniform. As attractive as the colorless white fabric was, I would *not* miss it.

Vincenzo was leaning against the wall, watching the entrance like a hawk. His body stiffened when he saw me stepping through the threshold.

"Riley." His deep voice sent shock waves through my core and reverberation against my bones. "Are you okay?"

Words failed me as my mouth opened and closed like a fish out of water. I thought I had expressed every emotion while trapped inside the box I'd occupied the last several weeks, but I was wrong. Vincenzo must have read the myriad of emotions rushing across my face. Stepping forward, he wrapped his arms around me. It was like a dam bursting, and years of contained water were spilling free from its clutches. My body shook with sobs as he held me. Lost in the safety of his arms, I didn't realize he had led me outside.

"Get in, Tesoro."

I slid into the cool leather seat of an SUV, still feeling detached from my body. The lights of Vegas streamed by the car, blurring against the setting sun. I pressed my hand against the glass and let the coolness of the pane calm the tumultuous nerves rattling my body.

"We're home, Riley."

My head turned toward his voice, my eyes locking with his. The deep color of his iris drew me in.

"Are you okay? Do I need to call a doctor?"

"No… it's just…" My voice tapered off as I searched for the words. "*Surreal.*"

Vincenzo reached out and brushed his thumb down my cheek.

"I know. This is my fault, and I will spend the rest of my days trying to make it up to you, but first…" He pushed open his door. "Let's get you inside. Michael called everyone to the house to discuss the next steps."

Vincenzo shut his door and stalked around to my side. The door opened, and he reached his hand in to take mine. Lacing my fingers with his, I eased out of the car. My legs felt like lead as I followed him inside. True to his word, everyone was waiting. Five sets of eyes pinned me to the floor.

"Riley." Madison rushed toward me, engulfing my body in the tightest hug.

Vincenzo's hand tightened around mine, reminding me he was close by.

"I'm so glad you're home. Are you okay? Did they treat you alright? How's the baby?"

"Madison," Massimo growled at his fiancée. "Give her some room, for fuck's sake. She just walked through the door. Let's not overwhelm her."

Madison released me and stepped back. "Shit. I'm sorry. I've just been worried about you."

"No." I smiled at her. "It's alright. To answer your questions, yes, I'm fine. I was treated as expected, and"—my hand instinctively went to my belly— "everything else is fine."

"Riley." Massimo wrapped his arm around Madison, who had settled against his formidable frame. "There are no words that can express the gratitude my family has for you for what you did. You risked everything to protect my brother, and for that, we will be forever in your debt."

I shook my head. "I'm not sure how much I've done."

"Are you serious?" Antonio had been leaning against the wall, silently watching me. "You ended Dmitri Ivanov. That alone puts you on a pedestal for life… sorry, Mads." He smiled at Madison. "You're still my favorite sister-in-law-to-be."

"Well, I guess there is no time like the present to tell you guys."

"Tell us what, Tesoro?" Vincenzo's fingers held on tight to mine as he pulled me toward him.

I glanced at Michael, who nodded.

"We need to fill you in on some new details. Details that will explain why she is being charged with manslaughter."

"I thought you said it was all for show?" Vincenzo ground his teeth together and pulled me against him.

"That was before this new information came to light." Michael retrieved a folder from his satchel on the table and handed it to Massimo. "It would appear Madison killed an innocent man."

"Bullshit!" Vincenzo roared beside me.

"Calm down, please." I tugged against his hand. "Just listen."

Massimo opened the folder and read the contents. His brow furrowed with confusion as he flipped through the documents.

"I don't understand." He glanced at Michael. "What does this mean?"

"It means Dmitri Ivanov is not dead."

"What?" Antonio grabbed the folder and shuffled through the contents. "You've got to be kidding me."

"Someone tell me what the fuck is going on, please." Vincenzo looked at me. I know he could see the strain on me. I felt as though I was ready to pass out. He led me to the couch and eased me down. "Sit down."

"It would appear I stabbed Donat Ivanov—Dmitri's twin brother."

"He had a twin?" Madison gasped. "How did we not know this?"

"Your partner, Jackson, gave me a little information about what they know. Apparently, they were estranged until recently. Donat fell into some trouble in South Africa, and Dmitri bailed him out. His repayment was to warn you. I guess he didn't see the flaw in his plan, or maybe he did. Either way, the Feds are saying Riley killed a man with no record."

"Even though she was acting in self-defense?"

"Yes, even though that is the story she gave. They want to make an example out of her."

"You mean punish her for loving me?" He sat down next to me and blew out a big breath.

My hand pressed against his leg when I sensed the turmoil he was feeling.

"Look at me," I whispered. My voice cracked with emotion as I fought back the tears when he shook his head. "Please, Vin. Look at me."

When he finally looked up, his eyes were filled with regret.

"I've allowed my shit to taint you, Riley. How can you sit there and look so calm? What happens if the charges stick? You'll be in prison. *Prison.* Do you understand?"

"I have faith that your family will keep me out of jail. But aren't you worried about the fact that Dmitri Ivanov is still alive? I killed his brother. Surely he'll want retribution for that."

"I promise you… he will not lay a hand on you." He brushed a loose strand of hair from my face and cupped my cheek. "All the people in this room would take a bullet for you, Riley. You're part of the Anastasi family now."

"He's right. And starting today, you and Madison will have a personal guard with you at all times if you're not with one of us. We will not risk either of your safety." Massimo nodded toward Donny.

"I've assigned Anders to you, Riley, and for you, Madison, Drew will be your personal guard. They will be at your side at all times unless you are at home with them." He pointed between Massimo and Vincenzo.

Everything had fallen apart, but I knew this man would spend an eternity to piece it back together for me—and our child.

When he placed his hand on the slight swell of my belly, I smiled.

"You're carrying my child. My life is irrelevant now. The only thing that matters is your life and the life of our son."

I hated to hear him speak as if his life had no value, but I forced a smile.

"A son, huh? I think it's a little too soon to know."

"Actually," Catarina interrupted as she stalked in through the door and slid in beside Donny. "You're what? Four months?"

"I think so. The jail wasn't exactly helpful in the matter, and I hadn't yet gone to the doctor before being arrested. I think I'm about sixteen weeks, though."

"Then you can find out the sex, if you want to."

"Vin?" I cut my eyes toward him, my unspoken question hanging in the air.

"I will do whatever you want, Tesoro. If you are ready to find out, then let's do it, or if you would rather wait until we are married, we will wait."

My eyes grew wide. "Married?"

"Yes, as soon as possible. If I had my way, we would've driven straight to a chapel and wed, but Massimo insisted this was more important."

"You assume I would say yes. Though…" I quirked a brow as I sat up straighter in the seat. "You haven't really asked."

The others in the room cleared out, leaving us alone. Vincenzo slipped his hand into his pocket and retrieved a box.

I thought he'd been joking when he said he planned to drive straight to a chapel. Easing off the couch, he slipped between my legs and kneeled in front of me, then pulled my hand into his and rubbed the soft flesh beneath my thumb.

"Riley, I believe people are put in our path for a reason, and sometimes, defying all odds, it turns out to be the best thing to happen. You are that person to me. Everything says we shouldn't be together. The path was turbulent from the start—both of us hiding secrets that could inevitably destroy us—but we led with our hearts and didn't let it keep us apart. I shouldn't have fallen in love with you. I should have guarded my heart better. The truth is, I worried my darkness would engulf you and taint your purity. Instead of clouding you in black, you lifted me up in light. You've changed me into the man I want to be. Without you, the air I breathe is poison. Will you take a chance on me? Will you give me your heart to protect and become my partner in life?"

He opened the box, revealing the sparkling gem inside. Vincenzo held my eyes as he slipped it onto my ring finger, waiting anxiously for me to say something. The tears trickling down my cheeks had him paralyzed with fear, waiting for the impending rejection. Glancing down at the band glittering on my finger, I cupped his cheek.

"Vincenzo," I whispered as I leaned forward and pressed my lips to his. My arms wrapped around his neck as I dominated his mouth with mine. Breaking the kiss, I rested my forehead against his. "Yes. I'll marry you. I can't imagine life without you."

He pulled me against my chest and buried his face into my neck.

"I love you, Tesoro."

I ran my palm down his back. "Vin."

"What is it, baby?" He leaned back, pressing kisses to the hand that now adorned his ring.

"Take me to bed."

twenty-seven

VINCENZO

"Are you ready?"

"Yes." I squeezed Riley's hand as we stared at the doctor.

He pressed the wand against her belly and watched the screen.

"Interesting."

"What?" I leaned in, trying to make sense of the grainy images on the screen. "Is there something wrong?"

"No. It's not that. Give me a moment." He moved the ultrasound around, searching for something. "I thought so." Smiling, he turned the monitor toward Riley and me.

"Congratulations, you're having twins."

"I'm sorry… what did you say?" Riley glanced at me. I was frozen to the spot, my face surely ashen and gray.

"You're having twins. Fraternal from the looks of it. See this?" His finger pointed to a blob on the monitor. "This is baby one's amniotic sac, and there is baby two. And these…"

He turned on the sound and a rapid thumping filled the room. It sounded like a pair of hooves moving in rhythm across the pavement. "These are their heartbeats. You are going to give birth to two healthy babies in about four and a half months. From the measurements, they are right on track and growing as they should."

Twins.

"Riley." I brushed my lips across her knuckles. "You've given me everything I don't deserve. Doctor," He looked up at him. "Can you tell what they are? I mean, their gender?"

"Yep. You're having one of each."

"A daughter and a son." The tears trickled down my face like a parade of happiness. "Wow, I can't believe this."

"I'll let you get dressed. I want to see you back in four weeks unless you have any issues."

"Are there any limitations in what she can do?" I helped Riley to her feet, holding her steady as she slipped on her shoes.

"Not as of now. She is in healthy shape, and her pregnancy shows that. Keep up the diet and exercise you're currently doing. Only stop something if you experience pain. Otherwise, no restrictions." He winked at me, causing Riley to blush.

"I can't believe this. I didn't expect to walk out of here today having two babies. Are you okay with things?"

"Of course. This is amazing, Riley. But there is one thing I want you to do for me."

She turned to face me. "What's that?"

"Marry me today. I can't wait another moment to make you mine permanently."

"Today? Are you serious?"

"Yep. It's Vegas. We can go to a chapel right now and make this union official."

She mulled over my words. Her hands drifted to the tiny bump swelling beneath her shirt, and I watched as her face split into a massive grin. I knew she didn't want to bring these babies into the world unwed—at least, I hoped she didn't.

"Okay, let's do it."

"Perfect. Anders," Vin barked at my guard, who had been waiting in the car. "You're going to be our witness. Take us to the Tiny Chapel on the strip."

"Wait." Riley tugged my hand. "Don't you think you should call your family? Won't they want to be there?"

"I'm not waiting around for them. We can have a real ceremony once the trial is done, and you're exonerated. This is just for us."

She slid into the car beside me, clinging to my hand. We pulled into the chapel parking lot and stopped.

"Now is the time to tell me you're having second thoughts, Tesoro."

She smiled, the light in her eyes beaming like a ray of sun. "Let's do this."

I pushed open the door and got out. Lacing my fingers in hers, we headed inside.

Despite the looming threat of Dmitri Ivanov or the fact Riley could still be found guilty of murdering Donta Ivanov, I felt nothing but happiness. The risk was there to lose it all, but I knew beyond any doubt, I would protect my family until my last breath.

The ceremony didn't take long and before I realized it, my wife was seated beside me in the car.

"We should probably go to Discoteca and talk with Massimo." Riley beamed, holding her ring up into the light.

"Yeah…" I tugged her against me. "How about I take you home first? You look exhausted."

When we arrived, Madison was seated at the bar. "Hey. How'd the appointment go?" She smiled, walking toward Riley.

"It went great." Riley sat down on a stool and sighed. "What's a girl gotta do to get a drink?"

"Oh, hell no." Madison shook her head. "I've been waiting to hear the verdict."

"I'll leave you two alone." Leaning down, I pressed a kiss to her neck. "I'm going to spill the news to my overbearing big brother."

I heard Madison squeal as I knocked on Massimo's door.

"Yeah?"

I peeked my head in and smiled. "Massimo, you busy?"

He waved me in. "No. Everything good with the baby?"

I nodded my head. "We got married."

"You did what?" Massimo growled.

"We got married." I paced the floor of his office. "She's having twins, Fratello. I'm going to be a dad."

"But marry her? Like that? Fuck. Mother and Father are going to be pissed."

"We will do it again, the right way when the trial is done. Any word on how that's coming?"

Massimo grinned and shoved a tumbler of whiskey into my hand.

"Antonio said he's making progress, but you know it's going to take time. I don't know." Massimo leaned back in his chair. "I feel like Antonio is hiding something. He's just been acting weird the last couple of weeks."

"Maybe sending him in like this was a bad idea. What if it backfires? I mean…" I took a sip from the glass I was holding. The amber liquid burned deliciously as it went down my throat. "She has to know he's an Anastasi. I can't believe she hasn't fired him."

"Me either. He claims she threatened to do just that, but something happened, and she changed her mind. Antonio is confident she will cave and give in to his demands. All we need is for her to drop the charges."

"I hope he knows what he's doing." I set the glass down on the desk and headed toward the door. "I'm going home with my wife. I just wanted to tell you my news."

"Congratulations, Vin."

I found Riley and Madison engrossed in conversations about our impromptu nuptials and smiled.

"I hate to interrupt, but I'd like to take my wife home."

Once we managed to get away, I rushed us home. I scooped Riley into my arms, making her squeal.

"Vin. Put me down."

"Absolutely not. I'm carrying you over the threshold." Riley giggled as I pushed open the door. As soon as I stepped through the entryway, her stomach let off the most obnoxious sound. "What the…" I glanced down at the swell of my babies.

"Oh, my God." She covered her face. "I'm sorry…"

I set her on her feet. "You hungry, baby?" She bit her lip and nodded. "Shit. I should have stopped and grabbed something. How about I run to the restaurant and grab something to celebrate our Elvis wedding?"

"Can't you send Anders, and *you* stay with me?"

"I sent Ander's home." I smiled. "I promise it won't take long. I'm going to lock up. Promise me you won't open the door for anyone. In fact, go take a bath or a nap—when I get home, we'll *celebrate* properly."

Leaving my new bride was nearly impossible, but I drove like the dickens and found myself at Bellissimo in no time. I hurried inside, heading straight to the kitchen. The place wasn't very busy, and I was able to get to the back without being stopped.

After explaining what I needed, Kevin, one of the line cooks, packed up two meals to go. I grabbed the containers and smiled.

"Thanks, Kevin. Let everyone know the both of us will be unavailable for a few days. I'm leaving you in charge." Once I was certain I had everything, I turned on my heel and headed out the back door.

I pulled the door shut and headed toward my car. Lost in thought, I didn't see the shadow stalking up behind me. Strong hands wrapped around my neck, jerking me back.

"You should have walked away." The thick Russian accent had me stiffening beneath my assailant's hands. "This is for Donat. Dmitri said your pretty little lady is next."

The tip of something sharp pressed into my neck. Hot, searing pain ripped through my body as he jerked the blade from my flesh. The food I'd been holding fell from my hands and the contents scattered across the ground as I reached up and clawed at my throat. Warmth from the blood seeped out of the wound trickled down my body and between my fingers.

The Russian released me, letting my body drop to the ground. His boot dug into my ribs as he gave me one last kick before leaving me to bleed out on the pavement only a few feet from the back door of my restaurant. My vision swam as my eyes fought to stay open. Pressing my palm against the gash in my skin, I used all the strength left in me to push myself to my feet. I couldn't leave Riley like this. I wasn't ready. Stumbling my way inside, I lost my balance and fell to the floor.

"Help me."

I tried to rasp out, begging for anyone to hear me. Blood littered the hallway, pooling beneath my body as I lay there, dying. I could feel my body giving out on me as the world closed in around me. How had I, the mighty La Lama, fallen so easily?

Once a formidable man the world feared, I had been reduced to a bloody heap. My brain conjured up images of Riley, flashing our life through my mind like a movie projector.

Had I told her I loved her enough?

Would she know how much my heart was filled with her?

"Shit! Vincenzo," the faint voice of someone whispered inside my mind. I didn't know if it was real or not. Maybe the visions of my life had conjured up the sound of him. Hoping they would be heard, I forced out the words. Riley needed to know how sorry I was to leave her like this.

"Tell…" I struggled to speak. My eyes refusing to open. "Riley I'm sorry."

I TOOK A QUICK BATH, my mind set on surprising Vincenzo when he returned. I pulled on his button-down shirt and hurried back downstairs. He'd been gone a little over an hour, so I expected him home any minute.

"Massimo?" I blinked, coming to a stop when I found him standing in my kitchen.

His voice cracked with emotion as he reached out toward me.

"Riley."

"What is it?" My heart raced as I watched Massimo shift on his feet. "Why are you here? Vin ran to the restaurant to grab dinner."

"Something's happened. Vincenzo was attacked."

"Attacked?" I repeated, not grasping what he was saying.

"It's bad, Riley. I need you to come with me."

Unable to move or speak, I just stared at him. He had to be wrong. Vincenzo was on his way home.

"You're wrong. He promised he'd be right back."

"Riley." He stepped forward and gripped my arm. "Please. I need you to get dressed. We have to go."

He guided me to the living room and sat me down. He must have grabbed some pants, because the next thing I knew, he was pulling a pair of Vin's sweats up my legs. "Here, stand up." He tugged them up, securing the tie at my waist. Shoving my feet into a pair of flip-flops, he guided me from the house to his car.

It wasn't until we pulled into the emergency room parking lot that I fully understood the gravity of the situation.

"We're here." I glanced out the window, surprised to see Madison rushing toward me.

"Oh my God, Riley. I'm so sorry." She extended her hand and helped me out. "Let me walk with you."

"Can someone tell me what's going on?"

"Massimo didn't tell you?"

"He just said Vincenzo had been attacked. Is he hurt?"

"Oh, Riley," Madison sobbed. "He's not going to make it."

Her words struck me like an arrow through an apple. My whole body seized up, and I stopped in place.

"What did you say?"

"The doctors said we needed to get the family here. They don't think he will make it through the night."

My knees gave out as the air left my lungs. "No."

Thankfully, Massimo was there to catch me, or I would've face planted onto the concrete. He guided me into the busy hospital and through a set of doors. I leaned into him as we climbed into the elevator and ascended toward the floor they had moved Vincenzo to.

"What happened?" My voice echoed against the metal walls.

"Someone stabbed him in the neck. It nicked his carotid artery, causing him to lose a significant amount of blood. I don't know how he did it, but he went back inside Bellissimo. Kevin found him just as he collapsed. I'm sorry I didn't call you sooner… I just—"

I held my hand up, silencing him. "No. Don't apologize. You did the right thing."

"They did surgery to repair the damage, but the blood loss caused too much damage. They don't think he'll wake up."

"I don't believe them. He wouldn't die on me… on us." My hands pressed against the swollen reminder of our future.

The hall was filled with forlorn faces as we stepped off the elevator. Antonio and Michael were leaning against the wall, huddled up and talking in hushed voices. Catarina was wrapped in Donny's embrace, her sobs reverberating through the waiting area.

"What about your parents?"

"They're on their way, but it takes hours to get here from Italy. I fear they won't make it in time."

"*Shut up*," I screamed. "Just Shut up. He isn't going to die." I fought back the tears threatening to rip through me. "I need to see him."

Massimo nodded and led me down the narrow corridor. He stopped in front of a closed door and sighed.

"He looks bad, Riley. Prepare yourself."

Swallowing, I forced a nod. I needed to see it for myself. Massimo pushed open the door and stepped across the threshold. Taking baby steps, I followed him inside.

Nothing in a million years could have prepared me for what awaited. Vincenzo was hooked to every machine made. He had a breathing tube protruding from his neck, right above his chest. The rest of his throat was wrapped in gauze, hiding the knife wound. I moved to the edge of the bed and pulled his hand in mine.

"Vin, if you can hear me, I'm here, baby."

The door opened, and a young doctor joined us in the room. "Mrs. Anastasi?"

"Yes." I whimpered, nausea threatening to make me throw up as I looked back over to my husband's still form.

"I'm Doctor Hicks. I need to tell you about your husband's injury."

"Okay." He pulled a chair beside the bed and helped me sit.

"Your husband suffered a stab wound to the left side of his throat. The blade penetrated his esophagus just below his eardrum. He was lucky in the fact it didn't damage his ear. Unfortunately, it's why we've inserted the vent where we did. Mrs. Anastasi, Vincenzo lost copious amounts of blood, restricting the oxygen to his brain. Right now, he's in a coma —but the reality of him waking up is low."

"Is he brain dead?"

"No, but his brain activity is lower than we want it to be."

"What does that mean?"

"Essentially, your husband could have brain damage. Right now, the vent is the only thing keeping him stable."

"Fine. Then we wait."

He blew out a breath. "Do you understand that could be hours or it could be years?"

I closed my eyes and swallowed. "Yes. I understand."

I listened as the doctor spoke to Massimo. I didn't care what he thought. I knew Vincenzo would do everything in his power to come back to me, so I'd wait.

"Riley," Massimo called out to me. I could hear it in his tone that he thought I should say goodbye, but I wasn't going to.

"I'm not leaving him, Massimo. So, don't ask me."

"I know you want to be here with him, but think about your health, your baby's health. This stress can't be good for you or them."

"You know what can't be good for them?" He cocked an eyebrow at me. "Having no daddy. Leave me alone. I'm not going anywhere. Not until he walks out of here with me on his own two feet or in a body bag."

"I'll see if they can bring in another bed." Massimo squeezed my shoulder. "You don't need to be sleeping in that chair in your condition."

The door snapping shut made me jump. I tugged Vin's hand into mine and squeezed.

"Baby, please wake up. I don't want to do this alone." I tugged his palm against my stomach. "We need you. I need you. We haven't even had a chance at happiness. This can't be the way our story ends. Come back to me, Vin."

The creaking of the door irritated me. I didn't want to be bothered by anyone.

"*What?*" I snapped.

"Sorry, Riley. I just need to ask you a few questions."

Looking up, I rolled my eyes when I saw it was Jackson.

"Why are you here, Jackson?"

Massimo crowded in behind him. "You need to leave."

"Look. I don't want to be here anymore than you want me here, but I need to ask some questions."

"It's okay, Massimo. Go ahead, ask your questions, then get the fuck out."

Jackson nodded. "Does this mean anything to you?" He held up a card with some sort of emblem drawn on it.

"*Fuck.*" Massimo whispered as he ran his hand down his face. "That's Dmitri Ivanov's calling card."

"That's what I thought. Riley." Jackson took a step forward, but Massimo put his hand out, stopping him. "I think you're in danger."

"You think? My husband is lying in a hospital bed, clinging to life. I killed Dmitri Ivanov's twin brother. This is not a coincidence, Jackson. When are you going to realize this is all connected?"

"I…" he stammered. "Look, I get it, Riley. I don't think you're guilty of manslaughter. I would have gladly put a bullet in Dmitri's head, too. But you screwed up and killed an innocent man."

"Get out." I turned back to Vincenzo's still form.

"Riley."

"I said, *Get. Out.*"

"It's time you left." Massimo pushed him from the room, leaving me alone with Vincenzo again.

I laid my head on the bed next to him and sobbed. If he died, and I was found guilty, my children would grow up without both parents. I needed him to pull through. If I was in jail, at least they would have him.

"Oh, Vincenzo. What am I going to do?"

twenty-nine

RILEY

One month.

That's how long Vincenzo had been in the hospital. His stats were improving every day, but he still hadn't woken up, making the doctors fear the worst—brain damage. I, on the other hand, believed he was just choosing to rest until he was fully healed. His parents had been here since the day after his attack. They've been a true godsend. His mother made sure I was fed and clothed, and his father kept the restaurant running. I had no idea he could cook like Vincenzo, but he claimed it's the Italian blood in him.

"Italians are born to cook, fuck, and kill," he said. "That man will wake up and make sure he does all three for you, Riley. Do not lose the faith."

It was easier said than done. The doctors ordered me to bed rest. They said the stress of everything caused some blood pressure issues, making them want to tether me to a bed. Thankfully, I demanded to be in the room with Vincenzo. I refused it any other way.

Somehow, Michael was able to get my trial delayed for another month. He swears the prosecutor took pity on my situation and agreed to postpone the hearing. I believe Antonio had something to do with her sudden change of heart. No one had seen him in a week. He assured us everything was alright, and he had everything under control, but I'm not so sure he's telling the truth. Like everyone else, they walk on eggshells around me.

I pressed my palm against the round protrusion beneath my breasts and watched in amazement as the skin beneath it rolled. Smiling, I tugged Vincenzo's hand from the bed and held it beneath mine. The twins were always active, making my insides feel like a jungle gym, but when I placed his hand there, they went wild. A soft thump against our entwined hands made me smile. It's like the babies knew when Vincenzo was touching me.

"That's your son or daughter. They can always tell when your hand is on my stomach."

I glanced up at his motionless body. The gauze had come off, leaving only a small square on his skin. They'd even removed the vent, saying he was breathing fine without help. His neck was still black and blue where the knife penetrated his skin. The doctor said it would heal and fade in time.

"My trial got delayed. I think Antonio has something to do with it, but no one tells me anything. Michael thinks this incident will have the jury on my side. It's kind of hard to argue we, or I, weren't in any danger. This proves Ivanov had malicious intent. Vin, what are you waiting for? Come back to me."

"How is he today?" his mother's voice cut through the silence as she stepped inside.

"Same."

"You need to take a break. Go. Walk. Shower. Eat something."

"No, I don't want to leave his side. Plus... bedrest, remember?"

"Hogwash. A little walking won't kill you. At least go shower, Riley. He wouldn't want to see you looking so... depressed."

"But I am. I need him to wake up." I wiped a lone tear from my cheek. "I can't do this alone, Giorga."

"Child." She pulled a chair beside me. "You aren't alone. You're an Anastasi now, and that means you have a big family by your side."

"I know." I shook my head. I didn't want to seem so ungrateful, but I *needed* him. "It's just not the same."

"We can't replace him. He's my son. But you'll never be alone, Riley. I promise."

"Why would she be alone?" The soft whisper had me nearly falling over with shock.

"Vincenzo! Oh my God." I stood and pressed my body into his. "You're awake." I sobbed uncontrollably, my body shaking with tears of relief.

"I'll get the doctor." His mother rushed from the room.

"What happened?" He rasped, his voice a mere squeak.

"You don't remember?" I held his gaze as he shook his head slightly in response. "You were stabbed."

His eyes widened as the memory assaulted him. He closed his eyes and sighed.

"I remember now. Someone jumped me in the alley behind Bellissimo. I thought…" He took a breath. "I thought I died."

The next few minutes were a flurry of activity. The doctor checked him over and drew blood. Massimo, Donny, Catarina, and his father all shoved into the room. Everyone was relieved he had finally woken up.

"Where's Antonio?" Vincenzo asked, scanning the room for his missing sibling.

"He's tied up right now."

"The prosecutor?"

Massimo shared a glance with Donny. "You could say that."

"Any word from Dmitri? Do we know if he did this to me?"

"We are fairly sure he did. The FBI found his calling card near the scene."

"Great. Something else for them to use against us."

"It's alright. I think Jackson is on our side."

"What makes you say that Massimo?" Vincenzo tried to sit up in the bed but collapsed when he realized it wasn't going to happen.

"Let's just say he came into a lot of damning evidence on Dmitri. The kind that makes careers."

"Let's go. Leave Riley and Vin alone." My father ushered everyone toward the door. "I am glad you are back, Son." He leaned down and pressed a chaste kiss to Vincenzo's head.

"Glad you didn't die." Catarina waved from the door and dipped out into the hallway. Donny nodded and followed her.

"I thought you were gone, Vin." I pressed a kiss to his cheek. "I don't know if I would have survived without you."

Vincenzo pulled me onto the bed with him and wrapped me in his arms. His palm rested on my abdomen as he leaned in and kissed me.

"I would move heaven and earth to come back to you every time, Riley. Nothing will keep us apart again. If I have to hunt down Dmitri when I am out of here, that's what I'll do. He needs to be wiped from this earth."

I snuggled in against him, careful not to tug out his IVs. He was right—Dmitri Ivanov needed to be wiped from existence, or he would continue to wreak havoc on all of us. If Vin didn't kill him… I would gladly put a bullet in his head myself.

"Where are we on your trial?"

"It's been postponed for a month."

"Okay." He pressed a kiss to my head.

"I hope the trial happens before these babies come. I don't want to be in jail giving birth without you by my side."

"You won't. I have to believe my brother's absence means he is making headway."

"I hope so." I snuggled into his hold, thankful to have him here with me.

"Have faith, Riley. Everything will come together as it's supposed to."

"Faith is the only thing that kept me sane."

"I'm sorry, Tesoro. I broke my promise never to hurt you. From this day forward, I swear to make your life one you deserve."

"I don't care about any of that as long as I have you." I closed my eyes and listened to his heartbeat. The sound was full of promise and hope for a life we deserved to have. "I love you, Vincenzo."

"E ti amo, Tesoro." The warm sensation of his lips pressed against my forehead. "Today is the beginning of our forever."

epilogue

ANTONIO

Two Months ago.

"Are you alright?" Michael's smooth voice cut through my thoughts.

"Yeah. Just reading over this file you gave me." I thumbed through the papers, looking for something to use against Rachel. She hadn't learned I was working in her house yet, but any day I would be found out, and I needed something. "There has to be something here I can use."

"You need to take a break." Michael pressed his palm against my shoulder. "How about I order some pizza?"

I glanced up at his face and froze. His eyes were the brightest green I'd ever seen on a man. They had a magical power that seemed to trap me inside their tiny orbs. My body reacted in ways I wasn't sure I understood.

"Yeah," I gritted out, uncomfortable with my reaction to another man. This wasn't the first time my body felt some-thing for a member of the same sex. Bastian had done something similar to me when I'd been in Chile. He showed me things I didn't expect to like. Not with a man.

Turning my attention back to the folder, I read a page of notes Donny had gathered on her. Alec had managed to hack into her personal accounts.

"Holy shit," I whispered, my eyes not believing what I was seeing.

"What?" Michael set a glass of whiskey down in front of me.

"I think I found something." I handed him the photo buried beneath the stacks of account information. "Looks like she has a semi-shady past."

"This? It's just a photo of her." Michael turned the image on its side. "A pretty naughty image, though. How's this going to help us?"

"I think our girl might have a fetish I can exploit."

My cock strained against my jeans when I thought about her in the photo. Michael must have had the same reaction because he adjusted his pants. My eyes tracked his movement as he palmed the bulge in his slacks. I couldn't take my eyes off his dick.

"Antonio?" Michael whispered my name. It was a whimper, if not a plea.

"Michael. I'm…" I swallowed, unable to finish my words.

He reached down and cupped my cheek in his hand. "Don't." He leaned down and pressed his lips to mine. His tongue licking at the seam of my mouth. Giving in to the carnal need for his touch, I opened to him. Our tongues met in a frenzy as he dominated my mouth. Gripping my shirt, he tugged me to my feet. His hands wound into my hair and held my head in place.

"Tell me to stop and I will," he uttered against my lips. Everything about this felt wrong, but I couldn't stop.

"Don't stop." I pressed my palm to his crotch and rubbed. His hard cock sent electric shock waves through my veins. "I think I'll go mad with need if you do." Gripping his shirt, I tugged him through the house to my room. Shutting the door, I grinned. "Are you sure *you* want this?"

"I've never wanted anything more."

Michael pulled his shirt over his head and tossed it on the floor. His chest was a well-defined slab of hardened muscle. I watched in fascination as he stripped his pants off and stood completely naked before me. The dark trail of hair paved a path toward his cock, which stood proudly on display.

"Are you going to just stand there?"

I quickly disrobed and pushed him to the bed. He pulled my arm, causing me to fall onto the mattress beside him. His fingers danced across my arm and trailed across my chest.

"Have you done this before, Antonio?"

I looked at him and smiled. "Yes. Once. Until a friend showed me it was okay to accept myself for who I am, I was afraid. You could say he enlightened me."

"Are you gay then?"

"Bisexual, I think. I like women, too, but my need for a man is strong. It's why I haven't settled down. Most men can't handle my need for a woman, and vice versa."

"What if I told you I could?"

My cock throbbed at his words. Everything about him had me worked up for weeks, but because I was afraid of what my brothers would think, I buried this part of me… until now.

"I like fucking women, too,"—Michael wrapped his fingers around my shaft and pumped his hand— "but there's nothing quite like a cock to get my dick hard as steel."

I should have been focused on Rachel's file. Lying in bed with my sister-in-law's attorney was a bad idea, but as his hand glided across my rigid member, I could think of nothing else.

"What about Rachel? We should be focusing on finding dirt on he—" My words cut off as he wrapped his mouth around my shaft. The heat of his lips sent my hips bucking off the bed. "Fuck," I gritted out, thrusting my body into his throat. The head of my cock pressed against the back of his throat as he bobbed his head along my dick. He made an audible pop sound as he pulled his lips from my crown and smiled.

"I want more."

I nodded, still stuck in a state of bliss. I wanted more, too, and knew exactly what to take from him. I shoved him onto his stomach and pressed between his legs. Lifting him to his knees, I rubbed the globes of his ass. My hand trailed down his hip and around his side. Fisting his cock in my palm, I jerked his cock.

"You're mine from this point forward. Do you understand?" I whispered in his ear, the heat of my breath tickling his neck. He grunted in response, his throat whimpering with need. "Say it. I need to hear it."

"I'm yours, Antonio."

Reaching to my nightstand, I pulled a bottle of lube and a condom from the drawer. Once I had myself sheathed, I poured the clear liquid between his cheeks. His body flinched from the cool sensation as it dripped down his thighs. Pushing a finger into his ass, I leaned forward and kissed his back. My cock was aching so badly, I wasn't sure I would last long. My hands gripped his cheeks and pulled them apart. I pressed forward, my bulbous head pushing against his star. He looked over his shoulder, watching with anticipation as I eased my cock into his backside. His moan nearly did me in as I seated myself inside him fully.

"Oh God," he moaned, jutting backward against me. "Fuck, you feel good buried inside me."

I held my breath, trying to control myself. I wasn't ready to come yet, but every nerve was firing on overdrive. Slowly, I shifted, pulling my cock out and slamming it back in. I gripped his hips and pummeled inside him, my balls slapping against his as I did. Reaching around, I tugged his cock into my hand. His palm laced with mine, jerking himself off as I fucked him. Our rhythm became frantic as we raced toward our climax.

"I can't hold out much longer, Michael."

"Me, either. Come with me," he grunted.

I could feel his muscles tensing around my shaft, signaling his orgasm was close. With a final tug of my hand, his cock exploded. I followed close behind, my own orgasm ripping through my body. Hot spurts of cum coated my hand as I filled the condom with mine. Our heavy breaths filled the room as we collapsed onto the bed.

"Holy shit," Michael whispered as I pulled out of him.

"Yeah," I mumbled.

The reality of what I had done hit me like a ton of bricks. I just slept with the family attorney—a man. What would Massimo or Vincenzo say? Shame riddled my core as I rolled off the bed. "You should go." I tugged the condom off and tossed it into the wastebasket as I walked toward my shower.

"What?" Michael leaned up, looking at me with confusion.

"You should leave. This was a mistake."

Michael hurried off the bed and stood before me.

"What are you talking about?"

"I shouldn't have slept with you. If my brothers find out…" I pressed my eyes shut. "Please. Just go. We can't tell anyone what happened."

"You're a coward." I could hear him shuffling around in the room. "I know you felt something just now. Don't deny it, Antonio."

"Please. I can't."

"Can't. Funny… it felt like you did. I guess the big bad man is afraid to admit who he is. That's a shame." The sound of the bedroom door opening had me opening my eyes. "When you're ready to admit how you feel, call me."

I watched as Michael stormed out of the room. Sliding to the floor, I sat with my knees drawn to my chest. Why couldn't I be like my brothers? Why did I want him so much? I closed my eyes and drifted back to the picture of Rachel. I couldn't help but wonder if… No, it wasn't possible. I shook the thought from my mind and stood. I needed to forget what happened with Michael and focus on bringing Rachel down. Everyone was counting on me to save Riley. Michael would just have to wait, but when I was ready—I hoped like hell he would still be there.

DOES ANTONIO STOP RUNNING FROM WHO HE REALLY IS? FIND OUT IN THE THIRD INSTALLMENT OF THE ANASTASI FAMILY SYNDICATE: Fatal Love

spotify playlist

about dori

"Love, Loyalty, and the Occasional Gunshot."

Dori Pulitano, a USA Today Bestselling Author, is the naughtier, much dirtier half Author LC Taylor. Writing men in shades of grey, the bad girl Dori embraces her Italian side with heroic hitmen, decadent conflicted dons, and oh-so-f*ckable assassins trying to trade their devilish ways for salvation —and the perfect woman to tie to their bed.

And F**k following the rules... this author is most definitely trigger-happy.

visit www.AuthorDoriPulitano.com to learn more.

facebook.com/AlphaBookBoyfriend

instagram.com/alphabookboyfriends

tiktok.com/@alphabookboyfriend

bookbub.com/authors/dori-pulitano